60p

Six Cousins Again

D0245266

Stories by Enid Blyton available in Armada

The Rockingdown Mystery
The Rilloby Fair Mystery
The Ring O'Bells Mystery
The Rubadub Mystery
The Rat-A-Tat Mystery
The Ragamuffin Mystery
The Secret Island
The Secret of Spiggy Holes
The Secret Mountain
The Secret of Killimooin
The Secret of Moon Castle
The Children at Green Meadows
Six Cousins at Mistletoe Farm
Six Cousins Again
Adventures on Willow Farm
Adventure Stories
Mystery Stories
The Mystery That Never Was
The Treasure Hunters
Shadow the Sheepdog
The Boy Next Door

Enid Blyton

Six Cousins Again

Armada

First published in the U.K. in 1950 by
Evans Brothers Ltd, London
This edition was first published in Armada in 1967
This impression 1988

Armada is an imprint of
the Children's Divison, part of
the Collins Publishing Group,
8 Grafton Street, London W1X 3LA

© Enid Blyton 1960

Printed and bound in Great Britain by
William Collins Sons & Co. Ltd, Glasgow

CHAPTER 1

The Six Cousins Talk

"LET'S all go over to see Holly Farm!" said Jane, on a fine December morning. "The Rokers have gone now. They went yesterday so it's empty."

"Yes, let's!" said Roderick and Susan, delighted. Melisande nodded too. She felt excited at the thought of seeing their new home.

Jack and Cyril came by the window, and the others yelled to them. "We're going over to see Holly Farm – the Rokers have gone. Are you coming too?"

The two boys opened the window wide enough to jump in. "What's all the shouting about?" asked Jack.

"Haven't you finished your Saturday jobs yet," said Jane. "We've decided to go and look at Holly Farm."

The six cousins began to talk at the tops of their voices. Jane and Jack were twins, getting on for sixteen. Susan was their little sister. She was twelve.

Melisande, Cyril and Roderick were their cousins. Cyril was sixteen, Melisande was fifteen, and Roderick was the youngest of the six cousins, even younger than Susan. They sat there, talking nineteen to the dozen, with Crackers, the black spaniel listening as if he understood every single word.

'We've been staying with you so long now that Mistletoe Farm seems like home," said Melisande, looking round the cosy, rather untidy sitting room. "I shall miss it."

"Yes – it's almost eight months since we came," said Cyril, counting up. "Our house was burnt down then, and we came to you."

They all sat silent for a few minutes, remembering that

5

far-off April evening, when the telephone bell had shrilled out, and the news had flashed through. Susan especially remembered everything clearly. She never forgot anything!

"Jane went to the phone first," she said, "then Mummy went, and we heard her saying she was horrified, and terribly sorry for you. We couldn't think what had happened."

"It seems a long time ago now," said Melisande. "I don't mind telling you we all three hated the idea of coming to stay with you – Mistletoe Farm seemed dreadful to us after lovely Three Towers."

"Well, we didn't want you either," said Jane. "None of us did – except perhaps Mummy, but she's always so sorry for people when things happen to them. I remember how I hated having to clear out a chest of drawers for you to put your clothes in, Melisande. I couldn't bear the idea of sharing a room with you. Well, I still don't like it, actually, but I've sort of got used to it."

"And Roderick hated that little room up near the cistern," said Susan. "You were afraid of the gurgles it made – do you remember, Roderick?"

"Gosh, yes – I must have been an idiot," said Roderick. "I never even notice the noises the cistern makes now."

"You'll probably miss them when you get to Holly Farm," said Jane, with a laugh. "I'm sure everything is absolutely up-to-date and well-behaved at Holly Farm – even the cistern! It seems funny to think you'll be moving in so soon."

"Yes – it'll feel strange to be only three of us instead of six," said Jack.

"Strange for us too," said Cyril. "But after all, we're not very far away. And if Dad can get us each a horse, we'll be riding over pretty often."

"It's almost four miles by the road, but it's only two-

and a half by the fields," said Susan. "That's what Twigg the poacher told me, anyway. He says he'll show me all the short cuts when you move."

For eight months the six cousins had had to live at very close quarters indeed with one another.

Mistletoe Farm was certainly not meant for six children – it was hardly big enough for three! It had meant sharing rooms, living on top of one another, and being altogether very uncomfortable.

Added to that, the three Mistletoe Farm cousins were real country children, and the other three whose house had been burnt down, were real town children, who turned up their noses at life in the country. So there had been quarrels and bickering and bad temper – but then somehow or other the corners had got knocked off, and now the six cousins were genuinely sorry to part.

"It's jolly decent of your father to buy Holly Farm for *my* father, and set him up there," said Cyril to Jack. "I guess Dad will be happy, running a farm himself. It's what he always wanted to do, but he just had to live in a town because Mother hated the country."

"She'll still hate it, I expect," said Susan. "But it's her turn to do something she doesn't like. Your father had years of living somewhere *he* hated."

Jane gave her a nudge. Susan was always so tactless. Melisande frowned.

"Don't talk like that about my mother," she said to Susan. "I wouldn't dream of saying things like that about *your* mother!"

"No, because she's not like . . .," began Susan, and got another, sharper nudge from Jane. Now it was Susan's turn to scowl. She never could understand why she couldn't always say exactly what she was thinking. And she was thinking that her beautiful, well-groomed Aunt Rose would most certainly hate to live on a farm and run a farmhouse! In fact Susan simply couldn't imagine her doing it.

Aunt Rose, the mother of Cyril, Melisande and Roderick, was so different from Susan's own hardworking, cheerful, sensible mother. Certainly Aunt rose always dressed much better than Susan's own mother, who was nearly always in overalls as she raced about the house doing the hundred and one jobs that were for ever waiting for her – and certainly Aunt Rose smelt nice and had pretty hair and walked almost as if she was floating on air.

But on the other hand Susan's mother, according to Susan, was the best in the world – she was a *mother*, and in Susan's opinion Aunt Rose wasn't a real mother at all. Hadn't she let all her three children live at Mistletoe Farm for eight months and only come to see them once? Susan opened her mouth to remind Melisande of this, and then shut it again. Jane would nudge her for the third time if she said anything more about mothers!

They all began to talk about Holly Farm. It had just come onto the market at the right time. At first the children of Mistletoe Farm had been afraid that their father was going to buy it for their own mother, because Mistletoe Farm was old-fashioned, and very hard to work. But their mother had said no she couldn't leave dear old Mistletoe Farm – and so Holly Farm had been bought for the cousins. Their father, brother to Susan's father, was to run it, and his wife, Aunt Rose, was to come down from Scotland, where she had been staying; and so once more the family, split by the burning down of their old house, were to be together again.

"Holly Farm's got electric light and gas," said Roderick. "That'll please Melisande – no more cleaning oil lamps and filling them!"

"And it's got a proper water supply," said Jane. "And

8

"They cantered off in the crisp, frosty morning. Jack looked back at Mistletoe Farm as he went."

Dad says the cows' milking shed is all tiled! Fancy cows having a place that's tiled. Do you suppose they like it?"

"I don't care if they like it or not," said Melisande "*I* shall like it. At least it will be easy to swill down and clean, and won't smell as horrible at the cowsheds here."

"They *don't* smell horrible!" said Susan, indignantly "Cows smell lovely."

"The stables are fine too," said Cyril. "Of course, they're new. The ones here must be very old. I shall like the new ones – but there's a kind of *feel* about the old ones here that I love."

"Yes," agreed Susan, "as if they're still remembering all the nice old horses that ever stood there. I know what you mean."

"Well, if we're going to have a squint at Holly Farm, we'd better go," said Cyril, getting up. "Come on – we'll ask your mother for the keys, and go over. You three ride on your horses, and we three will catch the bus that goes in ten minutes."

Cyril got the keys, and he, Melisande and Roderick went to catch the bus that went to the bottom of the lane in which Holly Farm stood. The other three cousins went to get their horses.

They cantered off in the crisp, frosty morning. Jack looked back at Mistletoe Farm as he went.

"I'm glad *we're* not going to Holly Farm!" he thought. "I'm glad Mistletoe Farm is ours. But Holly Farm will suit the others down to the ground. They'll love it!"

CHAPTER 2

Holly Farm

The three children on horseback got to Holly Farm before their cousins did. The bus had to go a roundabout way on the roads, but the three riders took short cuts over the fields. They arrived at the trim little farmhouse with pleasure.

"Let's tie our horses here," said Jack. "The stables may be locked. They'll stand at this gate all right. Susan, tie Boodi as far away from Merrylegs and Darkie as you can – I don't want him nibbling their tails!"

"All right," said Susan, obligingly. Boodi was her own pony, a real character. He had come from Iceland, and was like a little barrel, sturdy and strong. But he had several bad little tricks of his own, and one was nibbling the tail of any horse in front of him.

Susan tied him up a good distance from Darkie and Merrylegs. "All the same, I do think it's silly of the others to keep standing with their tails touching his nose," she said, giving Boodi a loving pat. "If *I* was a horse and knew Boodi, I'd always face him. I wouldn't give him a chance of nibbling my tail."

The three of them waited for their cousins to arrive, and soon they heard them coming up the lane. "Buck up" shouted Jack. "Come and have a good look at your new home."

Jane stood and looked at the pretty little farmhouse, where her three cousins were so soon going to live. It was whitewashed, and shone in the pale December sun. It was not so old and rambling as Mistletoe Farm, nor did it look so untidy, because the creeper on the house was neatly

11

trimmed, and flowerbeds nearby were neatly dug. The crazy paving paths were neat too, and not a weed grew in the cracks. No moss grew on the roofs, as it did at Mistletoe Farm, and not a scrap of ivy had been allowed to grow anywhere.

Holly trees and bushes stood all about. They had given the little farm its name. Trim holly hedges enclosed a square farm garden. Jane pointed to it.

"You'll be working there next year, Melisande, growing lettuces and radishes and parsley and mint, just like we do. And flowers for the house. It's not quite as big a garden as ours, so you ought to be able to manage by yourself, if your mother helps you."

For the first time Melisande's heart sank. She had helped in the garden at Mistletoe Farm – she had thinned out a few lettuces, and weeded a few beds. But now she suddenly realised that quite probably she would be the only one here at Holly Farm who would have either time or inclination to do the garden. A farm garden was always supposed to be women's work – no farmer dreamed of sparing one of his precious men to help with that. The farmer's wife and daughters did it.

And Melisande's heart sank because she felt sure that her mother wouldn't know a thing about the garden – and she, Melisande, would have to do it all by herself! Things wouldn't be quite such fun at Holly Farm as they were at Mistletoe Farm – there wouldn't be so many people to do them with, for one thing. And for another, who, except her father, would know *how* to do anything? Certainly her mother wouldn't know when to plant seeds, or how to thin lettuces.

"And what's more I don't believe she'll want to know," thought Melisande. Then she cheered up. "But after all, when Mother's really here, running this dear little place, she'll surely love to learn everything. I've quite enjoyed

12

all the things we did at Mistletoe Farm – though it's true that at first I hated everything. Oh dear – I do hope Mother won't hate things."

Cyril was looking with pleasure at the farmhouse, and the farm beyond. How well-kept – how neat and trim! Not a tile was missing from the barns, not a fence was broken anywhere. The hedges were well trimmed, the ditches were clean. It certainly was a model little place.

"I could almost run this myself!" said Jack, suddenly to his cousin. "It's in such shipshape order! Nothing to be mended, nothing to be altered – you've only just got to run it as it is. Your father's lucky, Cyril."

"Yes. And Mother will be lucky too," said Cyril, going up the neat path to the gleaming front door. "This will be play to run properly – not like Mistletoe Farm with its bad lighting and no hot water, and leaky roof. Let's go in and look."

Cyril pictured his pretty, smiling mother in Holly Farm. Surely it would suit her? He remembered his old home, Three Towers – his mother must have run that beautifully for there were always punctual meals, excellently cooked, the house was always shining and spotless, with lovely soft cushions everywhere, and well-swept carpets. He thought of the carpets at Mistletoe Farm.

"Worn and old, with holes you catch your feet in," he thought. "And dirty old cushions, because Crackers is allowed to jump on them, and the cats sleep there. And the curtains so faded. I've enjoyed my stay at Mistletoe Farm – but it *will* be lovely to have a *beautiful* home again, and well-polished silver on the table and things like that."

They were now inside the farmhouse. It wasn't really like a farmhouse at all – it was more like a town band-box of a house. The rooms were trim and small, most of them square. There were built-in cupboards in every bedroom so that no wardrobes would be needed – and to

13

Melisande's enormous joy, there were fitted basins there too!

She ran to turn on a tap. Water spouted out at once. "Look!" she said. "It's just like we had at Three Towers, Roderick – basins in our bedrooms. Look, Jane – won't you envy me, being able to wash in my own bedroom, and not even having to pour the dirty water away! No wardrobes, no washstands – my, this place will be easy to run."

It was completely modern. A gas stove stood in one corner for cooking. A boiler stood on the big hearth, excellent for heating water all over the house. Jane looked at it silently.

"I suppose all this *does* save a lot of work," she said, reluctantly. "But I do like our big old range at home, where Dorcas does the cooking – I love all her pots and pans and kettles on top, and the great big oven. It's nice to sit by too."

"You're old-fashioned," said Melisande, looking into the larder. "Look here – tiled all round too, just like the kitchen – and there's even a 'fridge! We can have ice cream whenever we want it!"

"Good," said Roderick. This was the first word he had spoken so far. He hadn't like the inside of Holly Farmhouse at all. It didn't feel right to him, after the friendly cosiness of the rooms at Mistletoe Farm. Everything here was so *proper*, he thought. He was sure he wouldn't like it as much as dear old Mistletoe Farm. Still – he would have his mother again. He had missed her very much, more than either Cyril or Melisande had. It would be lovely to have her back again.

He pictured her sitting at the head of the table at high tea each evening, just as his Aunt Linnie did at Mistletoe Farm. Aunt Linnie had a very nice face, he thought loyally, but his mother was so pretty, and her hair was never untidy like his aunt's. Yes, decidedly it would be lovely to have her here at Holly Farm, looking after him, and fussing him as she used to do.

The children examined the house and the farm thoroughly from top to bottom. The house was just big enough to take them all, if Daddy didn't have a dressing-room, but kept all his things in Mother's room, or out in the cupboard on the landing.

"Mother won't like that much," thought Melisande. "But I expect she'll soon get used to it. Roddy's got a dear little room – he'll like that. But he'll certainly miss his cistern!"

The barns were in excellent order, and so were all the sheds. What machinery the recent owner had left for Cyril's father to buy was gleaming like new in its own shed. There was a tractor there, and Roddy's eyes gleamed when he saw it.

"I hope Dad will let me drive that," he said to Cyril. "Is he going to have a car?"

"Of course," said Cyril. "He'll have to, to get to market and back, and fetch and carry things from the station."

There was no livestock on the farm at all. Mr Roker, the last owner, had taken it all with him to a bigger farm. Cyril's father was going to restock Holly Farm with the help of his brother at Mistletoe Farm. That would be exciting, Roddy thought.

"When do we move in?" asked Roddy. "I want to be here in good time for Christmas. I want to have my Christmas dinner here for the first time this year. When is Mother coming?"

"She's coming soon, with Daddy, to get the house ready for us, and to have everything shipshape for Christmas," said Melisande. "I wish it wasn't still term-time – it would be fun to help to get everything straight. Perhaps we could come over on Saturday and Sunday and do a few jobs ourselves."

15

They had spent about two hours wandering over the house and farm. Reluctantly they decided it was time to go home. "Though 'Home' will soon mean here, and not Mistletoe Farm!" thought Melisande. "It *will* be nice to have a home again – just our own family, and not anyone else – though I do like Jack, Jane and Susan. Still, we shall often see them."

She and Cyril and Roderick went off to catch the bus. The others untied their horses and cantered over the field-paths home.

"What do you think of Holly Farm?" asked Susan, after a while.

"It's nice – but it's a toy farm, not a real one!" said Jack. "Give me Mistletoe Farm every time!"

And on the bus Cyril was asking Melisande the same question. "What do you think of Holly Farm?"

"Oh, it's *lovely*!" she was answering. "It's not old and dark and overgrown like Mistletoe Farm. Give me Holly Farm every time!"

CHAPTER 3

Moving In

The next excitement was moving in, of course. Everyone at Mistletoe Farm was thrilled with this, not only Cyril, Melisande and Roderick. Even Dorcas got "all worked up," as she called it, and went over to see it she could do any scrubbing.

Mrs Longfield went with Jane to hang the new curtains that had arrived in good time. They looked very nice

16

indeed. "Aunt Rose certainly has good taste," said Jane, as she looked at the new hangings, half wishing that she had such pretty curtains at her bedroom window too. She didn't even know what colours hers were supposed to be, they were so old!

"Mummy, wouldn't *you* like some new curtains sometime?" she asked suddenly, watching her mother look admiringly at the blue ones she had just hung in Aunt Rose's bedroom.

"Yes. I'd love some," said her mother. "But things like that have to wait, if you run a farm there always seems to be something much more important to buy – machinery, or new hens, or feeding-stuff. I've kept meaning to make *you* some new ones, Jane – yours are the ones I had in my bedroom at my own home when *I* was a girl! It's a shame that I can't give you a pretty, dainty bedroom like Melisande is going to have. Especially now that you have got so much tidier in your ways!"

Jane grinned. She had had to share her small bedroom with Melisande for eight months and Melisande had grumbled bitterly at the way Jane scattered her things everywhere. She had even threatened once to throw Jane's "smelly old jodphurs" out of the window if she left them lying about the bedroom any more.

"Yes. I *am* better now," said Jane. "But I don't know if I'll be able to keep up my good ways when my bedroom is my own again, without Melisande there to grumble if I'm too untidy."

"Oh, don't say that, Jane," said her mother with a groan, unpacking some brown-red curtains for Cyril's bedroom. "It's been such a pleasure not to have to grumble at you so much. Dear me – how we shall all miss your three cousins now."

"Yes. But it will be lovely to have you all to ourselves again," said Jane. "I don't like sharing you with so many people."

"Don't I take enough notice of you, when I've six children instead of three?" said her mother, with a chuckle. "All right, you wait – I'll begin to notice all kinds of things when I've more time – your dirty shoes – buttons off. . . ."

Jane laughed. She climbed up on the window sill to slide the curtain rings on to the rod there. Out in the yard Roderick and Susan and Crackers were unpacking a big crate, performing peculiar feats with a chisel and a screwdriver. Mrs Longfield, looking down too, thought it all looked very dangerous indeed.

"I suppose they think they're helping," she said. "But all that will happen is that the chisel will slip and cut somebody's hand – or jab Crackers' nose. He sticks it into everything!"

They had planned to lay the linoleum and the carpets, and hang the curtains before the new furniture came in. It wouldn't take long then for everything to be straight, and Aunt Rose hoped to have the children in their new home at five o'clock on the afternoon of moving-in day.

"Who's going to help Aunt Rose?" asked Jack, wandering in to see how his mother and Jane were getting on. "Is she going to have somebody like Dorcas?"

"She's bringing someone," said his mother, shaking out another curtain. "And Dorcas has got her niece to come in every day and help. So Aunt Rose should be very comfortable indeed – she'll lead the life of a lady – quite different from mine! She'll be able to keep her hands nice, for one thing, and she'll be able to look pretty when Uncle David comes in from his work – which I never do when Daddy comes in! I'm always too busy!"

"Oh Mummy – why, I think you *always* look nice!" said Jane, surprised. "I'm sure Daddy does too – even if he doesn't say it. Anyway I'd rather have you than Aunt Rose any day."

18

"Sh!" said her mother, as Melisande came into the room, looking flushed and pretty with excitement at helping to get her new home ready. "Hello, Melisande – finished putting up Roderick's curtains yet?"

"Yes. And I've helped Cyril to put down the carpet in my room and in his," said Melisande. "Isn't it fun, Aunt Linnie? I'm just longing to move in."

"We'll feel strange without you all," said her aunt. "But it will be nice for you to have your mother and father again and be one united family. That's what families are meant for – to live together in friendship and love."

"Like yours, Aunt Linnie," said Melisande unexpectedly. "I wish we were going to live a *bit* nearer to you – not two or three miles away. I've a sort of feeling we'll want to keep popping in and out to ask how we do this and how we do that! It's a good thing Mother has someone she's bringing here to help – and Dorcas has got her niece to come. She couldn't manage like you do."

"Well, my dear, if you're in difficulties, you know quite a bit about household and farm affairs now, you and Cyril and Roderick," said her aunt. "You can surely help in all kinds of ways. You can't live on a farm like Mistletoe Farm for eight months without knowing a good deal of its running!"

By the time they left that day, Holly Farmhouse looked quite homely! The carpets down on the floor and the curtains hanging at the windows gave the house a friendly look. Melisande looked back at it, and felt very glad they were all going to live there.

"Daddy will love it," she thought. "He'll be really happy in the country. So shall I, though I never thought I would. How lovely to have Christmas Day in our own house!"

Moving in day came at last. It was on a Friday, so Cyril, Melisande and Roderick were all at school. They begged to help, but their father said no. "You'll be better out of the way!" he said. "Your mother's seen the house and she's got the plan of it. She has arranged exactly where all the new furniture is to go. We'll manage fine."

In great excitement the three children took a different bus from their usual one that Friday afternoon, rode in the opposite direction, and got out at the end of their lane. Up the lane they raced in the darkening evening. The sky was very clear, and the evening star hung low and bright. They crunched their way over frosted puddles, and looked out for the first glimpse of their new home.

"There it is!" said Roderick, suddenly, as he saw a light shining out from a window, and then from another. "Oh – it does look nice and welcoming! Mother will be there."

They raced in at the gateway and up to the front door. It had been left ajar for them. They tore into the little hall, feeling the warmth at once – for Holly Farm actually had central heating, and the whole house was warm from top to bottom. What a change from the chilly rooms at Mistletoe Farm!

"Mother! Where are you?" shouted Roderick, impatiently, and flung open the sitting room door. And there was his mother, sitting by a bright log fire, waiting, looking as young and pretty as ever.

The three children flung themselves on her, and both Melisande and Roderick thought the same thing at the same moment. "Why! We're bigger than Mother is now!"

Their mother gasped at the onslaught of the three hefty children, and pushed them back, laughing. "One at a time, dears! Melisande, how you've grown – and you really *are* fat! Cyril – you don't look the same!"

"Well – I've grown too," said Cyril, marvelling at the slightness of his mother.

"No – it's the way you've had your hair cut," said his mother. "It's so *terribly* short! We'll let it grow long now,

20

just as it used to be. And how is mother's boy, my darling little Roderick?"

Roderick was so delighted to have his mother again that he didn't even mind being called "mother's boy" He tried to sit on the arm of her chair, and hugged her.

"Oh dear – how you rumple me!" said his mother. "What enormous children I've got now. Well, how do you like your new home, dears?"

"It's *lovely*," said Melisande, at once, looking round at the sitting-room, and marvelling how different it was from the rumpled, untidy room she knew so well at Mistletoe Farm. "Oh Mother – it's so nice to have pretty cushions about again – and flowers everywhere – and the fire irons shining – and everything so tidy!"

"And a fine wireless!" said Cyril, joyfully. "I was hardly ever allowed to put the wireless on at Misteltoe Farm, because Uncle wanted to read the paper, or something. Even though he knew that Aunt Linnie might like to hear a concert!"

"He's such a boor, your dear uncle," said his mother's soft voice. "Well, you can turn on the wireless whenever you like now. This is your own home and you can do what you please. No cross uncle to say you mustn't do this and you mustn't do that – and no busy Aunt Linnie rushing round with a red face, sending everyone to do jobs!"

Roderick drew back a little. He was very fond of his Aunt Linnie. "She's awfully nice, all the same," he said, loyally.

"Oh, of *course*," said his mother, and pulled him towards her again. "But surely I'm the kind of mother you want, aren't I? Just look at me and see!"

They all looked at her. She laughed up at them, as pretty as a picture, her hair shining. The little pearly ear-rings in her ears caught a spark of fire-light as they swung.

"You look so *young*!" said Cyril. "And you smell so

nice – and you've got a pretty new dress on. Yes – you're the kind of mother we want!"

"But Aunt Linnie's nice all the time," said Roderick in a small voice. "You're much *prettier*, Mother – but Aunt Linnie *is* nice!"

CHAPTER 4

Teatime At Holly Farm

"Well, let's have tea," said Mrs Longfield, pushing Melisande away and getting up. "Ring the bell, dear. Everything's ready. We got straight so quickly, because you were clever enough to put up the curtains and put down the carpets for me. Daddy will be in soon, I hope. He's just gone round the farm – not that there's much to see yet."

The door opened and a maid came in. She looked very smart indeed in a black frock and frilly white apron. She carried a silver teapot and hot water jug on a silver tray. The children stared at her.

"These are the children, Ellen," said Mrs Longfield. Ellen gave them a stiff smile and a nod.

"Yes, Madam," she said. "Er – somebody's left the front door wide open. Shall I shut it?"

"I will!" said Cyril, and rushed out. They had all been so excited at coming "home" for the first time that nobody had remembered to shut the front door behind them!

"I don't like her much," said Roderick, when the door had shut behind Ellen, and her footsteps could be heard tap-tapping down the hall.

"Now you mustn't be awkward, dear," said his mother,

sitting down at the table, and lifting up the teapot. "We're lucky to have persuaded Ellen to come down to the country – she wouldn't have come if we hadn't had such a modern farmhouse."

Melisande looked with pleasure at the pretty teacloth, the plates with lace mats on them, and the silver teapot. It was a long time since she had seen such a dainty meal. She compared it with Mistletoe Farm – the big cloth that entirely covered the table and so soon got spotted – the great brown teapot – the plates covered with food, but with never a lace mat to grace them.

"It's lovely to have things nice again," she said. "I didn't know how much I'd missed all this kind of thing till I looked at this tea table. It's just like it used to be at Three Towers, before we lost everything in the fire."

"Yes – I was afraid you wouldn't like pigging it at Mistletoe Farm," said her mother, sympathetically.

"Well, dear, if it rests with me, we shall never "pig it" – we shall live as we used to live, even if we are in a much smaller place, and haven't so many lovely things."

Roderick was also surveying the table – but with very little pleasure. Silver teapots and lace mats meant nothing to him – what *he* noticed was the lack of food! Where was the dish of ham, the big fat scones, the great fruit cake, the round cream cheese, the big pats of butter that had always accompanied high tea at Mistletoe Farm? He was hungry, and didn't much like the look of the plate of thin-cut bread and butter, and the biscuits and little buns on this tea table. Why, he could eat the whole lot and still be hungry!

"Is this all we're going to have?" he began – and then someone tapped at the window, and a voice outside cried: "What a glorious sight! All my family together again!"

"Daddy!" yelled Roderick, and pushed back his chair so suddenly that it overbalanced and fell with a crash to the

23

floor. He tore out into the hall, followed by Melisande and Cyril. Soon their father was being hugged and squeezed, and everyone was laughing happily.

"It was a wonderful sight to see you all sitting round the table like that," said Mr Longfield, taking off his heavy coat and hanging it in the hall cupboard. "I must just go and kiss your mother before I wash. She looked like Melisande's sister, sitting there at the table. Rose, here I am! Welcome me to our new home!"

His wife smiled at him, pleased that he said she looked like Melisande's sister. But she noticed that his boots were dirty and his hands too, and she gave him a little push after his kiss.

"Go and wash, you dirty boy! And just you be careful never to come in smelling like your brother at Mistletoe Farm! Hurry up, and we'll all have tea."

Mr Longfield was soon back, and took his place, beaming. This was the first time for eight months that he had had his whole family together under one roof in a home of their own. He was delighted. He loved them all so much – and now he was going to lead the life he liked. He was going to be a farmer, and live in the country!

He looked admiringly at his wife. He was lucky to have someone so dainty and pretty – not like his brother's wife, Linnie, who seemed to go about all day long in overalls, and always looked hot and hurried. She had turned into a typical farmer's wife and he was glad that Rose showed no signs of it. He wanted someone decorative, someone whom everyone else would admire.

Roderick sat close to his father, glad to have him back again. He had taken a thin piece of bread and butter on to his plate, and doubled it up, – and then put it into his mouth whole! It really only made one mouthful and was gone in a minute.

"Roderick! You really can't eat like that now you're at

home with me," said his mother, horrified. "Oh dear – the children will have to learn their manners all over again, I'm afraid David. Their stay at Mistletoe Farm may have done their health a lot of good – thought I do think Melisande is much too fat – but how it has ruined their manners."

"Mother! How has it ruined mine?" said Melisande, hurt. "You want to see Jane's, if you really would like to know what bad manners are!"

"Jane has no manners at all," said her mother. "Neither has Jack. As for Susan – and that perfectly awful dog, Crackers . . ."

"Crackers isn't an awful dog," said Roderick swallowing a piece of bread-and-butter so quickly that he almost choked. "I'm going to miss him very much. Don't say anything against Crackers. And I say – is this all there is to eat?"

"Roderick dear – you're over-excited or something, I think," said his mother, in a gentle voice. "What else should there be to eat at teatime?"

"Well – ham – or eggs – and a jolly big fruit cake – and some of that lovely cream cheese," said Roderick, re-membering all the things he had had at high tea at Mistletoe Farm. "And perhaps sausage rolls – and pickles . . ."

"Pickles! Sausage rolls! At teatime!" said his mother. "Surely you didn't have those things at Mistletoe Farm!"

"Yes, we did. Every single day," said Roderick. "Didn't we, Melisande?"

"Yes. You see, they had high tea there, Mother," explained Melisande. "I suppose *we'll* have afternoon tea and then dinner later – or supper?"

"Of course," said her mother. "You'll soon get used to it. We'll simply have to get you back to proper ways again."

Roderick looked very gloomy. "I don't know how I'm going to last out till supper," he said. "I'm always so hungry when I get back from school. Wouldn't Daddy rather have high tea too? Won't he be hungry when he comes in?"

"I suppose it wouldn't be possible to have a more substantial sort of tea than this?" said Mr Longfield to his wife. "Farming's hungry work. I got used to a big meal about six o'clock or so, when I was farming up in Scotland."

"I do hope you don't expect me to do without all the nice ways I've been accustomed to," said his wife, looking suddenly tearful. "After all – I've come to live in the country, when I much prefer the town. That's a big thing for me to do. And if you want me to give up all the little ways I've been used to. . . ."

"No, dear, no," said her husband, hastily. "I wouldn't dream of it. We certainly won't have anything you don't want. You've had a hard time this year, what with that dreadful fire, and losing all your nice things, and having no proper home for months. You deserve to have your own way now."

"Besides," said Rose, looking more cheerful, "we have Melisande to think of. She really ought to have things done nicely. It would be a shame not to bring her up properly."

Having her own way, Mrs Longfield was prepared to be charming again, and things went smoothly. She could be very witty and amusing when she liked, and had a pretty, silvery laugh. She exerted herself to conquer everyone at the table, and succeeded. By the end of the meal they were all thinking that surely it was the best thing that ever happened, their coming to Holly Farm and being all together again.

Roderick still felt hungry, however, when he got up

26

from the table. He didn't like to say any more to his mother, so he went quietly out of the room and down to the kitchen. Perhaps Ellen would give him a bit of bread and cheese.

Ellen was sitting in a chair by the fire – reading. Out in the scullery someone was doing something, but Roderick couldn't see who it was. Ellen looked up as he came in.

"What is it?" she said, coldly.

"Have you got a bit of bread and cheese I could have?" asked Roderick, staring round the neat, small kitchen, comparing it most unfavourably with Dorca's big warm kitchen at Mistletoe Farm with its geraniums on the windowsill and its fat clock ticking away.

"What next?" said Ellen. "A bit of bread and cheese and you've just finished tea! Did your mother send you out for it?"

"No. I came because I didn't have enough to eat," said Roderick.

"Well, I'm sorry. But I don't encourage children in my kitchen, and unless your mother says you can have bread and cheese, I can't give you any," said Ellen. She returned to her reading, and Roderick, rather scared, tiptoed out of the kitchen.

He suddenly felt homesick for Mistletoe Farm, and his cousins and Aunt Linnie and fat, comfortable old Dorcas in the kitchen – and above all for Crackers! He didn't want to go back to the others. He went to the garden door, opened it and slipped into the dark garden. Roderick wasn't at all sure that he liked Holly Farm after all!

CHAPTER 5

Mostly About Roderick

There was a light in the window of the scullery. Roderick remembered that he had heard someone out there. Who was it? A friend of Ellen's?

He went to the window to see. At the same moment the backdoor opened and somebody came out with a pail in her hand. Roderick knew her at once!

It was Sally, a niece of Dorcas's, who had sometimes come to see her aunt at Mistletoe Farm. She was a plump, round girl of about seventeen, with cheeks like an apple and a mop of dark hair.

"Sally!" said Roderick, in a loud, delighted whisper.

She jumped. "Oooh, who's that? Why, it's you, Master Roderick! What are you doing out here in the cold?"

"Nothing," said Roderick, truthfully. "Except I was wishing that Ellen was Dorcas."

Sally gave a little snort. "They'm different as chalk from cheese," she said. "Miss High-and-Mighty would fall foul of Dorcas in two minutes. Did I hear you say you wanted a bite of bread and cheese? You wait and I'll get you some."

She disappeared and came out with a generous hunk of bread and cheese. She pushed it into Roderick's hand. "There you are. Dorcas would have done the same – she knows what hungry boys are like. If you want any snacks, you just come to me, not to Miss Sour-Puss in there!"

Roderick gave a small chuckle. Miss High-and-Mighty! Miss Sour-Puss! What lovely names for the haughty, sour-faced Ellen. He whispered his thanks to Sally and went off to eat his bread and cheese in a nearby shed. He began to think of Crackers the spaniel again, and wondered how many dogs his father would keep.

"Farmers always have to have dogs," he thought. "I hope Daddy gets his quickly. Then I could have one of them for my own."

He went back indoors again, feeling much better after his talk with Sally and his bread and cheese. He determined to ask his father about dogs as soon as he got a chance.

Ellen had cleared away the tea. The sitting room looked cosy and friendly, with the curtains drawn, and a big log fire sending up flames and sparks. It crackled loudly. His mother was sitting making a new cushion cover by the fire, and Cyril was fiddling with the radio in the corner. Melisande was trying to make up her mind to leave the cosy room and look at her bedroom upstairs. She hadn't yet seen it all nicely furnished.

Mr Longfield was reading the paper contentedly in an armchair. From time to time he glanced at his wife and smiled. He felt very happy. A home again – and all his family round him – and a farm outside waiting for him to tend it and care for it as best he could. He would cover his fields with crops, set cows in his pastures, have sheep on the hills, and hens in the yard. There was a fine pigsty too – with a tiled floor almost good enough for him to eat off! He was lucky to get such an up-to-date little farm.

"Have you been up to see your bedroom?" Mrs Longfield asked Roderick. "Do you like it?"

"I haven't been yet," said Roderick.

"Where have you been all this time then?" asked his mother. Roderick remembered that question of hers of old. She always liked to know where everyone had been and what everyone had done. He answered vaguely.

"Oh – I've just been wandering about." He didn't like to say he had been to ask for bread and cheese in the kitchen, and he certainly wasn't going to give Sally away.

"I'm going to see my room," said Melisande getting up at last. "Come with me and see yours, Roderick. You coming too, Cyril?"

"Yes," said Cyril. "I must say it's marvellous to be so comfortable on moving-in day. Everything arrived and unpacked and set in place."

"Except the pictures," said his mother. "Daddy is going to put those up tonight. I'll come up with you and see if you like your rooms."

They all went up together, and came out on a small, but fairly wide landing. Three doors opened off it, and round a corner was another door, leading to the bathroom.

"Here's my room," said their mother and opened the door, showing almost exactly the same kind of bedroom that the three of them remembered at Three Towers, though this one was much smaller. Everything was new and pretty, and the bedspread matched the curtains just as all the bedspreads had done at their old home.

"It looks just like you, Mother, this bedroom," said Melisande, revelling in the daintiness. "Quite different from Aunt Linnie's, isn't it?"

"Ugh! Aunt Linnie's room is dreadful!" said her mother, with a shudder. "So bare – and the bed so big and hard – nothing pretty in it all. The only drawback here is that Daddy hasn't a dressing room. He'll have to share my room for his clothes, and I don't like that at all. Now let's come and look at your room, Melisande."

All the other rooms were pretty and neat and altogether charming. Mrs Longfield certainly knew how to choose curtains, carpets, furnishings and furniture! Melisande was delighted with her room, which looked out on to the orchard – though by now, of course, it was too dark to see anything outside.

The boys liked their rooms too, though privately Cyril thought his was a bit girlish. He had been so used to sharing Jack's bedroom, with its bare boards, old curtains and old, battered furniture that somehow this new room of his seemed more suitable for a girl than for him. A soft carpet covered the floor, a silk bedspread covered the bed, and coloured towels to match hung by the basin. The lamp by his bedside was very pretty-pretty too – he could picture Jack grinning at it when he saw it.

"It's a lovely house, though it's so small," said Melisande. "Where does Roderick sleep?"

"There's a little stairway beyond the bathroom," said her mother, leading the way. "Ellen sleeps in a bedroom up there, and next to it, under the eaves, is a funny little room that used to be a boxroom. It will do beautifully for Roderick."

"Oh – I do hope it's next to the cistern!" said Roderick, to his mother's astonishment. "If it made a noise like that one at Mistletoe Farm, it would be nice and friendly. I should like that. It would remind me of my little room at Mistletoe Farm."

"I should have thought you wanted to forget that horrible little room, not remember it," said his mother, opening the small door at the top of the little stairway. Roderick gazed inside. He liked it enormously. It was a funny shape – all awkward corners and slanting ceilings. The window was set very low – why, the sill only reached his knees when he stood by it!

A low, built-in shelf ran along one side of the room. His mother had put some books there and a few toys saved from the fire. Roderick recognized them in delight.

"It's a *smashing* room!" he said. "The best one in the house." He looked out of the window, and just made out a tree that reached the windowsill "It's got a tree outside," he said. "Does my window look down in the yard? Oh, good – I shall be able to hear the cock crowing in the morning and the hens clucking and the pigs grunting – when we have them."

The others left him up in his funny little room, pleased that he liked it. Neither Melisande nor Cyril would have liked it at all! "We'd always be bumping our heads on those awkward corners and slanting ceilings," said Melisande. "And thank goodness he's tucked right away from us so that we can't hear his singing and whistling. He's awfully noisy sometimes."

Roderick felt happy in his little room. He thought how much Susan would like it. And Crackers too! Crackers would sniff into every corner, and learn the whole room with his nose. Then he would sit down on the mat and look round as if to say "Yes, it's a nice room. And if I lived here I wouldn't mind coming and sleeping with you on this little bed at night. Just in case you felt lonely."

It didn't do to think of Crackers. Roderick hadn't realised how fond he was of the little black spaniel with the melting brown eyes. If only, only he could have a dog of his own. What would he call it? Roderick went into a long dream in which names for dogs floated about, trying to find one for the particular dog he might have. But he couldn't think of one nice ènough for his dog.

He went downstairs at last and spoke to his father, "Daddy – farmers have to have dogs, don't they? Like Uncle has over at Mistletoe Farm. Are you going to have any?"

"Yes. The two I had up in Scotland are being sent down here," said his father, laying down his newspaper. "They're fine dogs – both mongrels though. I couldn't afford to buy pedigree dogs when I was working up there. You'll like them."

"What are they called?" asked Roderick, pleased.

"Punch and Pouncer," said Mr Longfield.

"They'll live in the house, won't they?" said Roderick, hopefully. But before his father could answer his mother spoke.

"No, of course not. Whoever heard of farm dogs being allowed in the house! They'll live out in the kennels."

"Daddy, can I have a dog of my own?" asked Roderick, feeling perfectly certain that neither Punch nor Pouncer would ever put a foot inside Holly Farmhouse.

"Well – I don't see why you shouldn't," began his father, pleased that Roderick, who had once been so afraid of dogs that he yelled if one went near, now wanted one of his own. But his wife interrupted at once.

"No, Roderick. You can't have a dog. Nasty noisy, messy creatures, covered in fleas!"

"Crackers never had a single flea!" began Roderick, indignantly. "I *wish* you liked dogs, Mother."

"I might get a cat, perhaps," said his mother.

"Pooh – a *cat*!" said Roderick, with the utmost scorn. "Who wants a cat? I bet there are dozens out in the stables anyway. There always are at a farm. Why can't I have a dog? I'd train it myself and I'd never let it worry you at all, Mother."

"Please don't bother me about a dog any more," said his mother. She saw Roderick's mutinous face and put out her hand to him. "What a dreadful face for mother's boy to put on the very first evening at home! Come here, darling."

But Roderick didn't come. He sat where he was, looking at the floor, sulking. He didn't want to be Mother's silly darling boy. He just wanted a dog.

CHAPTER 6

First Night At Holly Farm

It was fun to go to bed that night in the cosy bedrooms. It was lovely to have a hot bath and not have to carry up heavy pails of hot water, as they had had to do at Mistletoe Farm whenever anyone had had a hot bath. It was grand to switch on the reading lamp by the bed, instead of having to try and read by a guttering candle.

Melisande and Cyril took a long time undressing and messing about in their rooms that night. Both of them enjoyed the little luxuries of a soft carpet instead of bare boards with shabby thin rugs on them. Both of them liked to turn on the water in their basins instead of having to go and bang on the one bathroom door at Mistletoe Farm and yell to someone inside to buck up, they wanted to wash too!

The beds were soft and warm. The reading-lamps gave a bright, clear light, making reading in bed a pleasure. Melisande welcomed her mother warmly when she came in to say good night to her.

"Oh Mother – it's so lovely here, after Mistletoe Farm!" she said. "We *did* pig it there, you know! Now that I'm back in a decent place like this, I realize all I had to put up with – though the last few months I was there, I didn't seem to notice it. But this is something *like* a home!"

Her mother was pleased. She kissed Melisande good night and went in to Cyril.

"You must be very pleased to have left the hard life at Mistletoe Farm," she said. "I did feel so sorry for all you children having to stay there for so long."

34

Cyril was more loyal than Melisande. He remembered how hard his Aunt Linnie had had to work to look after six children instead of three for the eight months they had had to stay with her.

"I think perhaps it was good for us, Mother," he said. "It made me tough, you know – and I think I was a bit milk-and-watery before."

"Oh no, dear, you weren't," said his mother. "You were a well-mannered, well-brought-up boy – and there was no need for you to be tough! I want you to go back to your old nice ways now – and to begin with, dear, *don't* have your hair cut so short. It doesn't suit you."

"I'm not very keen on the kind of fellows who wear their hair long now," said Cyril, shortly. "And as for being tough – I'll need to be now if I'm going to help Dad on the farm."

"Oh, I couldn't allow that!" said his mother, shocked. "This is the first I've heard of such an idea! Why, you're only sixteen. You must go to school, of course – and perhaps to the university later – but you'll have to win a scholarship now, I'm afraid."

"I'm not clever enough," said Cyril, who had no illusions about his brains now. "I know I'm fond of poetry and music and reading and all that – but that won't win scholarships, just being fond of things! I've had to work harder since I went to Jack's school than I've ever had to work before, and I can see I've not got such good brains as any of the boys who win scholarships. So put that out of your head, Mother. I'm going to help Dad on the farm after this term."

His mother didn't argue with him. She felt quite sure that she could talk his father out of this idea, and persuade him to send Cyril back to school. She couldn't bear the idea of poor Cyril going on the farm so young – such hard work for him, too!

She said good night and went away. She wondered if Roderick was asleep. He had said rather a curt good night two hours before, and gone up to bed after making an enormous supper. She felt a little hurt. After all, Roderick was her youngest, her boy that she hadn't seen for so long. He had seemed to be the only one of the three who at all regretted leaving Mistletoe Farm.

She opened Roderick's door and went into the room without switching on the light. "Who's that?" said Roderick's voice at once.

"It's only Mother, darling," said Mrs Longfield, and went and sat on his bed. She stroked one of his hands, and wished he would put his arms round her as he used to before he went to Mistletoe Farm. He took his hand away.

"What's the matter, Roderick?" she said. "Aren't you glad to have Mother again?"

"Yes, of course," said Roderick. Then he burst out. "But if you were glad to have *me*, you'd give me a dog! What's the good of loving a person if you just won't give then what they want most in the world!"

His mother was startled. Roderick had never, never spoken like this to her before. Why, he sounded as if he didn't love her a bit! That's what came of letting him go to that awful Mistletoe Farm – he'd lost all his nice ways and nice talk. She debated what to say.

If she said firmly, no, he couldn't have a dog, he might sulk for days and spoil everything. If she put him off a little, she would soon win him round – after all, she had always been able to wind Roderick round her little finger. So she spoke gently to him.

"We'll see, Roderick. We'll just have to see."

"That means you won't give me one," said Roderick, at once. "Oh, I wish I was back at Mistletoe Farm with Susan and Aunt Linnie and Crackers. I shall go back there if I can't have a dog."

36

"Roderick lay and pictured Crackers' funny, mournful face."

"You're being silly," said his mother, shocked "You're just over-tired with all the excitement of the new house. Go to sleep now – and as I said, we'll see if you can have a dog. I'm not making any promises to a rude little boy."

She kissed him good night and went down the little flight of stairs, angry and disturbed. All this dog business! It would be bad enough to have two farm dogs rushing at her whenever she appeared outside, without having a tiresome dog in the house too.

Roderick lay awake, scowling. He knew he had been rude and unkind, but he was homesick for Mistletoe Farm. He wanted his Aunt Linnie. She didn't paw him about and pretend to be fond of him as his mother did – she really did like him and looked after him – she would have given him a dog, he knew she would!

And Susan would have said he must have one too. So

would Crackers, if he could talk. He *could* almost talk. Roderick lay and pictured Crackers' funny, mournful face, long black silky ears and loving, brown eyes. Now, if only he could have a dog like Crackers, he would be able to put up with anything at Holly Farm.

The cistern in the tiny box-like place next to his room gave a little gurgle. Roderick felt pleased. It sounded like Mistletoe Farm to hear that gurgle. He fell asleep listening for another gurgle, imagining that he was back in his room at Mistletoe Farm, with Crackers about to come into his room and jump on his feet.

Downstairs all was happy and peaceful. His mother and father sat beside the fire, happy to be together again. His father glanced at his pretty, young-looking wife with pleasure, thinking how fine it would be to have her here in the farm house looking after him and the children again. She would look nice even in the dairy, making the butter and setting out the bowls of cream. She would look nice feeding the hens. They would plan out the work together, and she would surprise him by doing it as if she had been country-born!

Mrs Longfield was pleased to have a home of her own again too. Of course, it was quite different from the lovely one she had had. Now she was a farmer's wife – but she would show everyone that it was possible to be a farmer's wife, and yet look pretty and dainty, and go to theatres and sit on committees just as she always used to do.

It didn't enter her head that her husband was expecting her to do any work on the farm. She had no thought of feeding hens, or grading eggs, and certainly not of washing them. As for making butter, well, she didn't even know how to, so that thought never occurred to her.

She sat there, peacefully sewing at the cushion, pleased with her good-looking husband, her "tough" Cyril, her pretty (though too-plump) daughter, and her youngest –

yes – pleased with him too even though he was so funny and obstinate. She would soon win him over.

Out in the kitchen Ellen sat reading by herself. She put down her book as the clock struck ten and got her hot water bottle. She yawned – a polite little yawn covered by her hand – not a vast, groaning yawn like Dorcas often gave, tired out at the end of the day.

She thought of Sally, who had gone home for the night, and was due to come back at seven the next morning. She didn't know whether she was going to get on with Sally or not. Sally was nothing but a rough, country girl without a thought in her head. Only seventeen too. Well, she would have to learn a few manners if she was going to share Ellen's kitchen.

As for those children, thought Ellen, she would keep them in their place from the very beginning. Master Cyril seemed all right '– quiet and nicely spoken. Miss Melisande might want too much waiting on. As for that Master Roderick, demanding bread and cheese immediately after a meal, well, she would soon stop that kind of thing!

She thought of her mistress. Mrs Longfield was gentle and sweet – there wouldn't be much trouble with *her*. Ellen liked her all right. Thank goodness there were no dogs rampaging about the house. She wouldn't stay a week if there were – messing up everywhere and barking and wanting food at all times!

Ellen slipped quietly up to bed. Now only Mr and Mrs Longfield were left downstairs. Rose looked at her husband. "Are you going to be up early, dear?" she asked. "That's the worst of being a farmer. You have to be up so early, and go to bed so early too. There never seems any evening at all, in a farmer's life!"

"Rose, dear, if you want nice, long evenings you can have them," said her husband. "*You* won't need to get up early. You can have your breakfast in bed. And even though I'll have to get up about six, I shall try not to wake you – and I'll stay up as late with you at night as you wish. I won't become a country clod, I promise you!"

Rose smiled. She hadn't very much liked saying that she would live in the country. In fact she had fought against it for a long time. But if she could get her own way in everything, it wouldn't be so bad. It would be easy to make everyone do as she wanted them to do – she had always found it easy!

But it wasn't going to be as easy as she expected. There were plenty of shocks coming to the little family at Holly Farm – shocks that not one of them suspected on that cosy, happy night when they were all together under the same roof once more.

CHAPTER 7

Saturday

The six cousins did not see one another over the weekend. Jack, Jane and Susan had been told by their mother not to visit Holly Farm on Saturday and Sunday, but to let their three cousins settle down in their new home. They wondered and wondered how they were getting on.

"Melisande will be so pleased to have that nice bedroom for her own, instead of sharing with me as she's had to do for so long!" said Jane. "But *I'm* pleased to have my room to myself again, I really am. It's nice to have got rid of all Melisande's bottles and jars and boxes off my dressing-table. *I* shall never want to use face cream at night like she does."

"Well, I rather hope you will, when you're old enough," said her mother. "You don't want to look like one of those weather-beaten, dried-up women, do you, that we sometimes see at the market? Why *shouldn't* you look nice? Daddy and I much prefer looking at you when you're clean, and your hair is shiny, and your nails are nice."

"So do I," said Jack, unexpectedly. "You did use to look simply awful, Jane. And you smelt too."

"She only smelt of horses," said Susan. "Who minds that?"

"Quite a lot of people," said her mother. "Anyway, even *you* sometimes say that your precious Crackers smells dreadful, when he's got wet out in the rain. So he does."

"Well, even if he does, I don't really mind," said Susan, hugging him. "Mummy, I bet Roddy's missing Crackers, don't you? Do you suppose Aunt Rose will let him have a dog? I'm sure she won't."

"I hope she *will*," said her mother. "I believe Cyril and Melisande would like one too – but Roddy really *needs* a dog – something he can love and call his own. He's a funny boy."

"I quite miss him," said Susan. "And I'm sure Crackers does. Crackers went up to the room by the cistern this morning, where Roddy slept, and sniffed all round like anything. He's awfully puzzled – he can't think why Roddy and the others have disappeared all together so very suddenly."

"Well, he'll soon see them again, I've no doubt," said her mother. "Now, are you going to clean out the hen-house for me today, or are you not, Susan? You said you would, so I imagine you are – but if you don't hurry up you'll have to rush over it, and I know you like to take hours and hours."

41

"Yes, I do," said Susan. "It's a nice job, cleaning out the henhouse. And I like putting down the peat on the floor afterwards – it looks so clean and brown. And I like putting new straw into the nesting boxes. The hens like me fussing round too – they all like to come into the henhouse to talk to me. And I talk back – like this. . . ."

And Susan gave such a very good imitation of clucking that an enquiring hen put its head in at the open garden door to listen.

"There you are!" said Susan, triumphantly. "See that hen? It came into see what I was saying in hen language."

"Go on with you!" said her mother, shooing Susan and the hen out together. "You cluck all day long, either in your own language or someone else's! Go and talk to the hens and the ducks – I've got work to do."

Susan wandered off happily, with Crackers at her heels, his long black ears brushing the ground whenever he put his head down to sniff at any exciting smell. Susan loved school – but she loved Saturdays too. There were so many nice jobs to do on Saturdays. She would clean out the henhouse – she would go round the farmyard and look under all the nearby hedges to see if any hen had laid away. She would count up all the eggs that had been entered in the eggbook that week. She would grade all yesterday's and today's into different sizes and wash them all. She would. . . .

And Jane was happy too, about quite a lot of things. She had got her bedroom to herself again. She had done quite well at school that week. She hadn't got a single order-mark against her form. She had all the weekend to mess about in. What should she do?

"I'll groom Merrylegs," she thought. "I'll groom him down to the last hair of his tail. Then I'll clean out his stable. Well, I might perhaps clean out all the stables, it's such a nice cold day. And I might go and have a try at

42

mending that bit of broken fence I saw the other day. I know where there's a bit of wood exactly the right size!"

Merrylegs, her pony, put his lovely head over the stable door as she came nearer. He whinnied softly. He adored Jane and she adored him.

"Hello!" she said, stroking his velvety nose. "You're the nicest animal in the world. And I'm going to make you look beautiful. No school today Merrylegs. It's Saturday."

Merrylegs knew that already, of course. All the three horses that the children rode knew when Saturday came. Jane opened the stable door and Merrylegs trotted out.

He was a bright chestnut pony from the New Forest. He had four white socks and a white star on his forehead, and was very loving and sweet-tempered. He swished his long tail, and nuzzled against Jane's shoulder.

Jane hissed as she groomed him. He liked that. Sometimes she whistled and he liked that too. Boodi, Susan's pony, put his wicked little head over his stable door and watched.

"I'm not grooming *you*, Boodi!" said Jane, severely. "You got loose yesterday at the stables where you waited for us to come out of school, and put your head in at a window and ate all the leaves off a plant standing on a table there. You're a bad horse, always into mischief!"

Boodi blew at her. He only really liked one person and that was Susan, though he had got used to Roderick too now. Jane would never ride him. He would gallop at top speed and then stop dead, just for fun, to see if he could throw his rider over his head. But he never did that to Susan.

Jack was happy too. He was glad to have his home and his mother to himself again, without his three cousins always demanding room and attention. He had gone up to his bedroom after breakfast and had rearranged the room completely, much to his mother's surprise.

"Merrylegs swished his long tail and nuzzled against Jane's shoulder."

"Well, Mother – I've felt it was Cyril's room more than mine, the last few months," said Jack. "All his books everywhere, and his bits and pieces. Now it's going to be mine and I've arranged it the way I like it."

Now he was out with his father, riding round the farm. His father rode his grey cob, Sultan, and Jack was on his own horse, Darkie, a Dartmoor pony with a black mane and tail. Jack liked these rides over the big farm with his father.

They looked at all the fields, lying brown and bare in the December sun, the frost getting at the earth and making it fine and powdery when the clods crumbled. They examined hedges to see that there were no gaps that the cows could squeeze through and get out on to the road. They looked solemnly at the herd of cows, and the cows looked back just as solemnly, chewing hard.

"They always look as if they were chewing gum, like the Americans do, don't they, Dad?" said Jack, and was rewarded by a guffaw of laughter from his father. They rode over to the hill where the sheep were. They looked well and healthy and their coats stood out round them, thick and curly.

"It's been a good year, Jack," said his father as they turned to ride back, after having a word with Hazel the shepherd about three sheep that were expecting very early lambs. "A very good year. That's how it was I was able to buy Holly Farm for your uncle."

"Suppose he has a bad year next year?" said Jack. "Will you lose money, Dad?"

"Yes. But he's a good worker, your uncle, and he understands farming, though living a town-life for years has set him back a bit," said his father. "It's your Aunt Rose that's going to be the making or marring of that trim little farm. She must help him. If she doesn't, he won't get far."

"Will Cryil help him too, Dad?" asked Jack. "Is he really going to leave school, as he said, and help on the farm. Why can't I leave too, and help *you*?"

"Because there's no need for you to," said his father.

"I've got good men – and I want you to learn to use your brains, so that when you do come on the farm, you'll never be at a loss. And I want you to go to a farming college when you leave, and learn all the up-to-date methods. You'll be more help to me trained than untrained!"

"Will *Cyril* leave school this term, though?" persisted Jack.

His father hesitated. "Well – there'll be no real need for him to," he said. "Your uncle's got a few good men, and when he gets his cows and sheep and pigs and the rest, and gets on to his planting, he should be all right with the labour he's got. But Cyril wants some sense knocking into him – he's too la-di-da for my taste. It would really do him good to knock about the farm for a bit."

"He'd have to wear good leather boots and gaiters then, and not sandals!" said Jack, with a grin, remembering how Cyril had worn sandals, and artistic shirts and flowing ties that year. "Still, Dad, Cyril's come on a lot since he lived with us. He's jolly good at football now too."

His father reined in Sultan to shout to one of his men who was spreading mangels over a field for the stock. Jack listened with half an ear, taking in the quiet fields and the distant hills and the view of the rambling old farmhouse not far away.

He glanced at the bare oak trees on which enormous clumps of mistletoe grew – the mistletoe that gave the farm its name. How many years was it since that mistletoe first grew there, planted perhaps by some thrush who scraped his sticky beak on a bough and left a mistletoe seed behind? How many years had his father, and his grandfather and his great-grandfather too, gone each Christmas to the oak trees, and got down mistletoe for the old farmhouse?

"I'd hate to have gone to Holly Farm," thought Jack,

for the hundredth time. "This farm is in my blood and I'll never leave it!"

"What are you dreaming of, Jack?" said his father, surprised at the serious, far-away look on Jack's usually stolid face. "Something nice, I hope?"

"Yes. Very nice," said Jack, but he was too shy to say what it was. Off they cantered together in the bright December sun, the horses' breath steaming in the crisp and frosty air.

CHAPTER 8

Roddy Goes By Himself

The next day, Sunday, the children's mother rang up Aunt Rose at Holly Farm. "How are you all getting on?" she asked, kindly. "I do hope you've settled in nicely."

"Oh *yes*," said Aunt Rose. "It's all quite perfect. The children are *so* happy."

"That's splendid," said Mrs Longfield. "We do miss them. I wondered if you'd like to come over to tea today."

Aunt Rose hesitated. A vision of high tea at Mistletoe Farm came into her mind – table loaded with far too much food, she thought – her own children gobbling and guzzling with their cousins – just as they had nicely settled in and she was trying to get back to better ways! No – it would be too upsetting!

"Well, dear, thank you for asking us, but I think it would be nice for us to be just ourselves here our first weekend," said Rose, in a cooing sort of voice. "I don't

47

really think any of the children would want to leave. They'll all see each other at school tomorrow."

Roderick was in the hall, and he heard all this. He leapt towards his mother. "Oh, let's go!" he cried eagerly. "It would be fun. Susan would love us to go, I know she would."

"Be quiet," said his mother, sharply. She was afraid that his Aunt Linnie would hear what he said. She turned to the telephone again and began to tell her sister-in-law all about the house. Roderick wandered away, disappointed.

Why *shouldn't* they go over to Mistletoe Farm to tea? There was nothing to do on Holly Farm yet – no hens to feed, no stock to look after, no milking to do – nothing interesting at all. A farm wasn't a farm till you had lots of animals about. Why, there weren't even any dogs!

"We could just as well have gone," said Roderick to himself, and he went out into the tidy yard and kicked a stone round and round it. He thought it would be very nice to have high-tea again too – there was always an extra special one on Sundays at Mistletoe Farm, because old Dorcas baked on Saturday afternoons, and her cakes and scones were at their very best on Sundays.

He considered things carefully. Would it matter if *he* went? He badly wanted to see Crackers. He went to find Melisande and Cyril, who were reading in the sitting-room. It all looked very tidy and proper, and the room was hot.

"Phew!" said Roddy, and opened a window. "It's stifling in here! Why don't you two come out? It's a lovely day."

"For goodness sake! Shut that window, you idiot," said Melisande, crossly.

Roderick shut it and sat down with a heavy sigh. Cyril looked up.

"What's the matter with *you*? I suppose you're mourning for Crackers!"

"Well, I do miss him," said Roderick. "Don't you? Didn't you like him awfully?"

"He smelt," said Melisande.

"So do you," said Roderick, rudely. "You've got scent on again. *Smell*isande!"

Melisande stared at her small brother in angry surprise. Cyril reached out and slapped him. "Get out," he said, curtly. "Go on – get out of here till you're in a better temper."

Roderick didn't move. He went very red and pursed up his lips. He knew he had been rude to Melisande and he felt rather surprised at himself. But he wasn't going to apologise after that blow.

"I told you to get out," said Cyril again. "If you've got anything sensible to say, say it, and clear off."

"I came to say that Aunt Linnie had telephoned to ask us all over to tea," said Roderick. "Do you want to go? Mother's refused for all of us."

"Well, that's that, then," said Cyril. "Anyway, I don't want to go. There's something I want to hear on the radio. I bet Melisande doesn't want to turn out on a cold evening, either!"

"No, I don't," said Melisande. "Do go away and don't bother us any more, you little pest."

"Would it matter if *I* went over to tea?" persisted Roderick.

"Poor boy – homesick for his precious Aunt Linnie and Susan and Crackers!" said Cyril with a laugh. "Go and ask, Mother. I bet she won't let you go. Who's going to get out the car for *you*, anyway, and run you over? And there's no bus on Sunday afternoon."

"I could walk there," said Roderick, gloomily.

"You don't know the way. Stop kicking at the carpet and do something," said Melisande.

49

Roderick wandered out, scowling. He wondered what Susan was doing. He wondered if Crackers had done anything funny or clever that weekend. You never knew what a dog like that would be up to. He wondered if Dorcas had baked any of the ginger cake he loved.

"I shan't ask Mother if I can go," he thought. "She'd say no and then she'd be cross if I disobeyed. I'll go without saying anything. I'll say *I* wanted to accept the invitation, even if the others didn't."

So that afternoon, about three o'clock, Roderick set off over the fields by himself. He hoped he would be able to find the way all right. He had to go across those fields by the stream, then up the hill and over it, and then make his way towards the wood. After that – well, he guessed he'd find out all right which way to go. So, with his thick coat on, and a scarf, and his rubber boots, he set off secretly. Nobody saw him go.

Teatime came and his father, mother, Cyril and Melisande sat round the tea-table. "Where's Roderick?" asked his mother. Nobody knew.

"He'll come along soon," said Mr Longfield. "He hasn't much idea of time. He's probably gone for a walk. I wish he'd told me, because I'd have gone with him."

Roderick didn't turn up at all – because he was miles away, stumbling over the fields, completely lost. He didn't know the countryside nearly as well as Susan did. She wouldn't have been lost. She seemed to have a nose like a dog, where direction was concerned. But poor Roderick had taken as many wrong turnings as it was possible for him to take, and now he hadn't the remotest idea where he was at all.

To make things worse, there didn't seem to be any house in sight, and he met nobody at all. And now it was almost dark! He began to get frightened.

He was also extremely hungry. He simply couldn't *bear*

to think of the laden table there would undoubtedly be at Mistletoe Farm. He stumbled on over marshy ground, trying to find some kind of a path somewhere.

"Ssssst!" said a voice suddenly, and Roderick almost fell over in fright. Then, to his enormous delight a wet nose was thrust into his hand, and something licked him. Was it – *could* it be – Crackers?

No – it wasn't. But it was somebody almost as good. It was the golden spaniel belonging to the old poacher, Mr Twigg. He called his spaniel by the ridiculous name of Mr Potts, after the village policeman.

"Mr Potts! It's *you*!" said Roderick, in delight, fondling the excited dog. Then Twigg himself loomed up in the darkness beside him.

"Why, it can't be *you*, Master Roderick!" said Twigg, in an amazed voice. "What's brought you out in these here fields this December evening? You're miles from home."

"Oh Twigg – I'm *so* glad to see you," said Roderick, in rather a shaky voice. "I'm afraid I'm lost. I set out to go to tea at Mistletoe Farm – and I suppose I didn't know the way."

"I reckon you didn't," said Twigg, and he took the boy by the arm. "Now you hang on to old Twigg, and he'll take you a short way home."

"Do you mean – to Holly Farm, or to Mistletoe Farm?" asked Roderick.

Twigg chuckled. "I reckon I mean Mistletoe Farm?" he said. "That suit you?"

"Oh *yes*," said Roderick, relieved. And he and Twigg set off in the frosty evening together, and were soon treading a path through a field, with Mr Potts trotting at their heels, his nose almost touching them. Twigg talked away as usual, and Roderick listened. Twigg was a bad old poacher, but he was very good company, and had a

51

heart of gold where animals and children were concerned – and what he didn't know about the countryside wasn't worth knowing!

"Your pa got his stock yet?" he asked after a bit. "That's a tidy little farm he's got – Holly Farm. Mebbe I'll come and call on you one day and get you to show me all the corners."

"Oh Twigg, *do*! Please do!" begged Roderick, delighted. "Dad hasn't got any stock yet, though, not even a hen. And we haven't got a dog, think of that – though Dad's having two sent down from Scotland. Punch and Pouncer. But they won't be as nice as Crackers or Mr Potts. Spaniels are the very nicest dogs, I think."

"Why don't you get one of your own?" asked Twigg. "Them that loves dogs are the ones to have them – good for them and good for the dogs too. How'd it be if I got you a pup one day – there's Tommy Lane's dog will have a litter soon – and a good little spaniel she is too, as golden as mine."

Roderick was so overjoyed at this idea that he came to a standstill and Mr Potts bumped his nose against the back of his legs. "Twigg! *Could* you get me one? I'd like it better than anything in the world." Then his face fell. "But Mother wouldn't let me. She hates dogs."

"You ask your Dad then," said Twigg. "If he says yes, I'll tell Tommy Lane and he'll save you the best little dog of the lot."

In a dream of joy Roderick stumbled along with Twigg, wondering how he could ever repay him for such a wonderful gift. He was amazed when he suddenly found himself at Mistletoe Farm, and the farmdogs came barking joyfully up to him.

"We're here!" he said, and tore up to the door he knew so well. Twigg grinned to himself and went round to the kitchen door to see if old Dorcas was in a good enough mood to give him a cup of tea and a slice of home-made cake with a bit of cheese to go with it.

Mr Potts, the spaniel, went with him, looking forward to a bone and a chat with Crackers. He liked Mistletoe Farm. It was a friendly, welcoming sort of place!

CHAPTER 9

Roddy Gets Into Trouble

It was just a quarter to six when Roderick opened the door and ran up the passage to the sitting room. He sniffed the familiar smell of Mistletoe Farm – a smell of log-fires, and stored apples, baking, and farm coats and boots stored in the hall cupboard. He burst open the door, and looked in.

Everyone was sitting round the table at high tea. They had just begun. The oil-lamp was set in the middle, giving off its usual mellow light. The log fire crackled and flamed. Crackers gave a sudden loud bark and leapt on Roderick, licking him from head to foot.

"Why – *Roddy*!" said his aunt, amazed. "Roddy! Are the others here too? I though you weren't coming. Your mother said no, when I asked you all to tea."

"There's only me," said Roderick, holding on to Crackers, and beaming round at everyone. "I wanted to come. So I came. What a lovely tea you've got."

"Come and sit down," said Susan, pulling up a chair for him. "We missed you, Crackers and I. And I think Boodi did too. How did you know the way?"

"I didn't," said Roddy, and told Susan and the others

how he lost his way and Twigg had found him. His Aunt Linnie cut him a slice of spicy ham and set it on his plate. She wondered if his mother knew he had come. Fancy starting out all by himself across the fields when he didn't really knew the way!

The telephone bell rang loudly and everyone jumped. Crackers barked. Jack got up to answer it. It was his Aunt Rose, of course.

"Is that you, Jack? Tell me, do you know where Roderick is? He didn't turn up for tea at half-past four, and we can't find him anywhere. I don't think he'd have been naughty enough to come over to you, but . . ."

"He *is* here," said Jack. "He's just arrived. And he's about to have a jolly good tuck-in, Aunt Rose!"

There was an angry silence. "How *very* naughty of him," said his aunt, in a most annoyed tone. "Not to say a word to any of us, either. He's to come home immediately Jack – immediately!"

"But how?" said Jack. "There's no bus till seven o'clock, and that's always crammed full with people coming back from the next village. He'd better stay the night."

Aunt Rose nearly had a fit. "Certainly *not*," she said. "He's a very naughty boy. He's not to stay to high tea – which is what you're having now, I suppose – and he's to come home at once."

Jack's mother took the receiver out of his hand. Jack was thankful. He didn't like dealing with Aunt Rose when she was in that kind of mood. His mother spoke soothingly into the telephone.

"It's all right, Rose. The child meant no harm – he probably wanted to see us all again, and that was very nice of him. I expect he missed Susan and Crackers a bit. We'll give him a good meal and keep him for the night."

"You'll do no such thing!" cried Rose, in anger. "I tell you, he's a naughty boy, and I won't have him fussed and pampered by you – slipping off like that so deceitfully – causing me all this worry. He never used to be like that – he's quite changed since he lived with you."

"Rose," said Mrs Longfield, warningly, "I can't have you speaking like that. Roddy's all right. And I shall most certainly give the child a meal – he's starving with hunger! But we'll send him back afterwards if you insist."

"I do insist," said Rose, in a trembling voice and slammed down the receiver. Mrs Longfield stood by the telephone, troubled. Silly, jealous, selfish Rose. She would have a lot of trouble with Roddy if she didn't handle him properly. Certainly he had changed – changed a lot, from a namby-pamby, scared little mother's boy, to somebody sensible and trustable, who knew his own mind, and was loyal to the people who had loved him and cared for him at Mistletoe Farm. Mrs Longfield hardly knew what to say when she went back to the sitting room.

Jack had shut the door so that Roddy and the others had heard very little. Roddy was looking rather scared now, but he was tucking in fast, all the same, afraid that he would be made to go before he had satisfied his hunger.

"Your mother was worried about you, Roddy," said his aunt, coming in. "You mustn't slip off without telling her another time. You must tell her you're sorry when you get back, and make things right again." She turned to her husband. "Could you run Roddy back in the car after his meal?" she asked. "I hate to turn you out on a Sunday evening – but would you?"

"Why can't David get out *his* car and come and fetch Roderick?" said her husband.

"Because Aunt Rose wouldn't *let* him!" said Susan, in her clear voice. "You know she wouldn't, Daddy."

"Be quiet, Susan," said her mother, exasperated by Susan's unerring habit of knocking unpleasant nails well and truly on the head. Roderick looked thoroughly miserable. He stopped eating.

"Pass Roderick a sausage roll," said Mrs Longfield, wondering how to manage a pert Susan, a miserable Roderick, and a scowling husband at one and the same time. She too thought that Roddy's father should get his own car and fetch him, instead of Mr Longfield bothering to do so on his precious Sunday evening. But what a fuss Rose would make!

Jane was sorry for Roddy, but she was glad he wasn't going to stay the night. After all, they'd only just got *rid* of their cousins – Jane didn't want any of them back again so soon. Susan wouldn't have minded, of course. She was fond of Roddy, and so was Crackers.

Roddy couldn't enjoy his meal after the telephone call. He dreaded going back home now. He couldn't make up his mind if Mother would reproach him and almost cry – or whether she would be cold and angry, as she knew so well how to be. She might tell his father to whip him. And his father always did everything Mother told him, then that would happen too. Roddy hardly tasted the delicious sausage roll, and even said no to a slice of ginger cake.

"Well, if you won't have it now, you must take it home with you," said his aunt, and wrapped up a large slice in a piece of paper. "Dorcas said yesterday when she was making it that she hoped you'd have a piece."

"Oh – thanks, Aunt Linnie," said Roderick, and put it in his pocket. He sat back and looked round. He hadn't known how fond he had got of this untidy cosy room. He looked at the picture of horses over the mantlepiece. He looked at the big basket of logs by the fireplace. He looked at the rosy face of his aunt, and for the hundredth time told himself that nobody else in the world had such kind eyes.

He looked at stolid Jack, munching away, and at Jane

with her mop of swinging hair. He looked at his uncle who had now retired behind a newspaper, holding it well up in front of his face because he was half afraid his wife was going to say something about the car again. He did *not* see why he should turn out. Let the boy stay the night!

Susan squeezed close to Roddy, and Crackers licked the two bare knees near his nose, one belonging to Susan, and one belonging to Roddy. "Did you miss Crackers?" whispered Susan.

Roddy nodded. "I wish you'd lend him to me sometime," he said beseechingly. "Just for one night – or perhaps two. Till I get used to Holly Farm."

"I couldn't," said Susan, at once. "You know I couldn't. I wouldn't lend him to the King of England."

"*He* wouldn't want him," argued Roddy. "But I do. I . . ."

Dorcas appeared at the door to clear away. Jane got up to help her. "I'll help too," said Roddy. "To pay for my lovely tea! Hello, Dorcas!"

"Well, here's a surprise!" said Dorcas, and ruffled his hair with her big hand. "And no wonder half the food's gone from the table, with *you* here again! How's my niece Sally getting on over at Holly Farm?"

"I don't know. All right, I think," said Roddy. "She's nice, Dorcas. I like her. She's like you a bit, I think, But she doesn't like Ellen. She told me so. I don't like her either."

Dorcas gave a sniff as she led the way into the kitchen, Roddy behind her with a laden tray. "Stuck-up piece she is!" she said. "I heard about her from the grocer."

Dorcas always heard about everything and everyone from the grocer, the laundry-man, and the postman. As soon as anything happened, old Dorcas knew it. She sniffed again and then rummaged about in the larder and produced two sausage rolls.

"You take these home with you," she said. "Sally's a good enough cook, but she don't make rolls like these."

"Oh thanks," said Roddy, thinking he was really doing very well. He put the paper bag of rolls beside the slice of ginger cake in his pocket.

In the sitting room an argument was going on. "You *must* take him home, dear," Mrs Longfield was saying to Roddy's uncle. "I'd love him to stay the night but Rose doesn't want him to."

"I don't care what Rose wants," said her husband, who had no love for his sister-in-law. "Why should I get out the . . ."

Goodness knows how the argument would have ended if there hadn't suddenly been an outbreak of hooting outside the house – it was Roddy's father who had got his own car out and come to fetch Roddy! Thank goodness! thought Mrs Longfield and ran to open the door and let him in.

"Couldn't let you bother to run him over," Roddy's father said to his brother. "Where's the little idiot? He's upset his mother properly. She didn't even want me to come and fetch him – said you were to bring him over. It's a pity this had to happen our first weekend."

Mrs Longfield thought secretly that before many weeks had passed many more things of a similar kind would happen, but she didn't say so. She called Roddy, kissed him goodbye and sent him out to the car. His father wouldn't stay a minute.

Roddy was very silent in the car. His father spoke gruffly but not unkindly to him. "You're to apologize to your mother. You're to have no supper. And you're to go straight up to bed. And remember, Roddy – Holly Farm is your home now, and you belong there and not to Mistletoe Farm."

"Yes, Dad," said Roddy, in a low voice. He did exactly

58

as his father said when he got home. He told his mother he was sorry, and listened to her reproaches without a word. He said nothing about supper, but went up to bed at once. He undressed and got into bed. Then he turned out his light.

He lay there for a while and then, when he heard the others at supper, he got out his two sausage rolls and his slice of ginger cake. Whatever anyone said, he was going to have *his* supper too. "And I bet it's a nicer one than they're having downstairs!" he said fiercely. But all the same poor Roddy didn't really enjoy it very much!

CHAPTER 10

Christmas Comes

The next day was Monday – school again. Roddy was very thankful and tore off immediately after breakfast to wait for the bus. His mother had her breakfast in bed, and he had tiptoed in whilst she was still half-asleep, given her a half-hearted morning kiss, and gone.

Cyril and Melisande had been very scornful about his little escapade. "Making us go hunting all over the place for you!" said Cyril. "And Mother thinking you'd been kidnapped or something. Pity you weren't!"

"I met Twigg," said Roddy, trying to change the subject.

"Pooh – that horrid, smelly old poacher," said Melisande at once. "You be careful of him. He'd better not start coming to *our* kitchen door. Ellen would soon tell him to clear off."

"Sally wouldn't," said Roderick.

"Sally's only a silly girl," said Melisande. "She's not very polite to Ellen, either. Ellen complained to Mother."

"*I* don't feel very polite to Ellen somehow, do you?" said Roderick. "She looks at me as if I was a bit of mud, or something. I daren't go into the kitchen when she's there."

Cyril came back to the subject of Roderick's escapade. He had very much resented having to turn out into the dark, frosty farmyard and hunt about for a Roderick who wasn't there. He said quite a lot about it to Roderick, who rapidly got bored and annoyed.

"Twigg says he can get me a spaniel like Mr Potts," he said, trying once more to change the subject.

"Mother'd never let you have a dog!" said Melisande at once. "*I* don't want one in the house either."

"What – not one like that lovely golden spaniel Twigg's got – Mr Potts?" said Roderick, amazed. He was sorry now that he had mentioned it. Melisande might go and tell his mother before he, Roderick, had sounded his father. He debated how to change the subject again. Fortunately for him the bus arrived at that moment and they all got in.

Melisande met Jane and Susan at school that morning. Susan ran up to her, pleased to see her again. "Hello! How are you getting on at Holly Farm? Do you like it? How's everybody?"

"We like it all very much," said Melisande. "You should see my bedroom, Jane and Susan – it's perfect. The towels have even got my intials on, and match the bedspread. And it's heaven to wash in a proper basin with running water. You really *must* see my bedroom."

"You ought to see mine now, too," said Jane, a little snappily. "I've got room to move about!"

"I don't have to wash up any more," went on Melisande, "or even lay the table. And even when the

60

hens come I shan't bother with them. As for cleaning them out – ugh – I'll never do that again!"

"Who's going to do them then?" demanded Jane. "I bet your father won't have time. And no farmer ever spares a man for silly work like feeding hens."

"Oh, something will be arranged," said Melisande airily. "Anyway, the thing is – you've just no idea what it means to be in a place like Holly Farm with running water and electric light and everything nice."

Jane and Susan soon got tired of all this. They left the excited Melisande and went off to their own friends. Melisande, although about the same age as Jane, was in a class below her, and soon she was regaling her own particular friends there with details of the model farmhouse she had now moved to.

"I hope she gets over it soon," said Jane to Marilyn, her own friend. "I sort of feel she's making more of it then she otherwise would just so as to make me feel that my own home, Mistletoe Farm, is down-at-heel and old-fashioned and shabby."

"Yes. That's rather like Melisande," said Marilyn. "Never mind – it's holidays soon, and maybe you won't need to see her much. I never did like her, anyway, though I tried to, because she was your cousin."

The holidays soon came, and then there was Christmas to look forward to. Mrs Longfield, at Mistletoe Farm, asked all the Holly Farm folk over to Christmas Day. At first Rose hadn't wanted to accept, because she wanted Christmas in her new house.

But Ellen didn't seem at all keen on doing anything extra for Christmas. Sally was willing enough, but Ellen told her mistress that, what with the move, and the new country air, she didn't really feel up to coping with big Christmas parties, so if Madam felt she would like to accept the invitation from Mistletoe Farm, she, Ellen, would be very glad.

"And seeing that Sally and I are both asked too, I'd be willing to give a hand there," she said, as if it was a tremendous favour.

Melisande and Cyril were disappointed, because they too had looked forward to Christmas Day at Holly Farm. But Roddy could have shouted with delight. He didn't, of course, because he had sensed his mother's jealousy of Mistletoe Farm, and said very little about it now. But his heart filled with joy when he thought of Christmas Day over at Mistletoe Farm.

"I bet Dorcas does wonders!" he thought. "I bet there'll be the biggest plum pudding in the world, and the finest mince pies. Gosh, it will be grand!"

It certainly was grand. Everyone went to church on Christmas Day, then they all met together at Mistletoe Farm. It looked beautiful, decorated with mistletoe from the old oak trees, and red-berried holly from many of the holly trees around. Old Man's Beard was twined everywhere too, like wool from grey sheep, and Susan had made strings and strings of tiny cardboard lanterns and paper-chains.

"It's lovely, Sue," said Roderick, admiringly. "Much better than ours. Mother doesn't like decorations much because she says they make such a mess. I say – what a wonderful smell from the kitchen. Do you think we could go out there? I've got a present for Dorkie."

Dorcas was bending over the enormous oven, her face as red as the berries on the holly round her big kitchen. She was basting the turkey. She slammed the oven door shut and beamed at the children.

"What's that? You've got a present for me, Master Roderick? Well, I never. What do you want to go and bother with old Dorcas for?"

"Because you're a very nice person," said Roddy, promptly. "I made it myself for you, Dorcas."

"It was a little carved figure that Roddy had made out of a piece of wood. He had carved a bird because Dorcas was fond of birds, and fed them every day. She admired it very much and put it up on the mantelpiece in a place of honour.

"I hope you'll enjoy the plum pudding, Master Roderick," she said. "You helped to stir it – do you remember?"

They remembered all right. "When I stirred it I was afraid Daddy was going to buy Holly Farm for *us*," said Susan, "and then we'd have had to leave dear old Mistletoe Farm. So when I stirred I wished and I wished we'd never leave Mistletoe Farm – and I made Crackers stir and wish too, didn't I, Crackers – and our wish came true."

"Now you go back to the others and leave me to getting the dinner for you," said Dorcas. "And could you take the old cat with you, because she does keep getting under my feet so. Put her down by the fire in the sitting room, and she'll purr away there like a happy kettle."

Roderick picked up the cat, and he and Susan and Crackers went back to the others. Roddy's mother was looking very young and pretty as she sat talking to some people who had called in. Mrs Longfield looked at her admiringly. How did she manage to keep so pretty and attractive? Mrs Longfield caught sight of herself in a mirror and sighed. Oh dear – her hair was ruffled again, and her face was red with hurrying to see to this, that and the other.

The Christmas dinner was magnificent "And no wonder," said Mr Longfield, beaming at his wife "You and Dorcas are the best cooks in the world! Goodness knows what you do with a turkey to make it taste like this. Isn't she a marvellous cook?"

"Rather!" said his brother. He turned jovially to his wife. "It a pity *you* can't cook like this, Rose," he said.

"The plum pudding was the biggest Roderick had ever seen."

"I've never needed to," said Rose, in a rather a cold voice. "And I hope I never shall."

"I shouldn't think you could boil an egg, could you, Aunt Rose?" asked Susan, in an interested voice. "*I* can boil an egg, and fry bacon, and make toffee and . . ."

"Really?" said Aunt Rose, in such a bored voice that Susan fell silent.

The plum pudding was the biggest Roderick and the others had ever seen. It came in surrounded by purple and yellow flames, all on fire. It was full of money – or so it seemed! Roderick got a sixpenny bit and a threepenny bit, Susan got a shilling, Melisande got a thimble, much to her digust, and Cyril got a threepenny bit. Roderick offered Jane his sixpence, but she wouldn't take it.

"Thanks awfully, all the same," she said. "But you have to keep what you find in puddings, you know."

"Well, I'll *buy* you something with the sixpence then," said Roderick.

Crackers, fruit, nuts, jokes – everything was just right for Christmas. Mrs Longfield was a good housewife and had forgotten nothing. Mr Longfield glanced proudly at her. His Linnie certainly worked hard every day – but whatever she did was very successful.

"She makes the best jam, the best pickles, bottles the fruit perfectly – and she's cheerful all the time!" he thought. He raised his glass and called out a toast.

"To Linnie – all our love – we couldn't do without her!"

The children raised their glasses of orangeade and lime-juice, and shouted at the tops of their voices.

"Mummy! My love!"

"Aunt Linnie – all the best!"

"Best mother in the world!"

"Best aunt too!"

"God bless you, Linnie," said Uncle David – and the only one who found it difficult to join in with pleasure was Aunt Rose. Would anyone ever toast her like that, with delight and joy and love? She couldn't help feeling just a little bit doubtful.

CHAPTER 11

Work At Holly Farm

"Can't *we* give a party, Mother?" asked Melisande, a little while after Christmas. She had very much enjoyed all the jollity at Mistletoe Farm. Everyone had, in fact, except Aunt Rose – and Ellen.

Ellen had not been a success in Dorcas's kitchen. Dorcas couldn't bear her "sourpuss ways," as she called them. She and Sally worked hard, joking and laughing, managing the old-fashioned range well. But Ellen turned up her nose at everything.

"What a place!" she said. "I couldn't stay here a week. That awful stove!"

"Maybe you wouldn't be wanted to stay for more than a week," said Dorcas. "Now, just hand me those tea cloths – land-sakes, can't you even wash up without being told? Sally, don't gape, child. Put another kettle on the stove."

No – Ellen had certainly not enjoyed herself. Dorcas hadn't been impressed by her fine, high-and-mighty ways, and Sally had giggled. Ellen had been very glad to get back to Holly Farm with all its trim neatness and plentiful hot water.

Now Melisande wanted a party. Well, why not? Her mother thought for a moment and then said yes, they would have one in February, when it was her birthday.

"Oh yes – it would be nice to have a party on your birthday, Mother," said Melisande. "Daddy would like that too."

"We'll show your Aunt Linnie that we can put up a much better party than she does!" said her mother. "We'll ask them all over here – and we'll ask all the neighbours too, and you can ask that nice boy – what's his name – the one whose party you and Jane went to in the summer."

"Oh yes – Richard Lawson," said Melisande, pleased. "He's got that wonderful horse, Lordly-One. Perhaps he will ride over on it and show it to Daddy. We'll ask his mother too. She's awfully nice."

Mrs Longfield was pleased to have a party to work for. She began to make all kinds of plans, though it was still a long way ahead. She would have this door taken off and that one – and so join up two rooms nicely. She would turn Cyril's room into a coat-room. She would have this food and that food, and order all kinds of things.

66

She told her husband about her plans. He nodded but didn't smile very much over the idea. "You'll remember, Rose, won't you, that we're not well-off now?" he said. "You can't give extravagant parties like the ones you used to give. You mustn't order this food and that from the London stores – it must all be done at home, just like Linnie does it."

"I didn't think you'd grudge me a birthday party," said his wife, looking like a spoilt little girl.

"I don't," said Mr Longfield, putting his arm round her. "But you know that our new cows and hens and ducks and sheep are coming soon, Rose, and they've got to be paid for – and wages have got to be paid too. I shall have a shepherd to pay and a stockman and an odd man too, you know – and there are Ellen's wages and Sally's. It's a lot to come out of a little farm like this."

"All right. I'll manage everything I can at home," said Rose. "I expect Sally and Ellen can get down to the cooking and baking. I'll have things like sausage rolls and ham – a sort of cold buffet."

Whilst Rose went ahead with her plans, Mr Longfield went ahead with the buying of his stock. His brother Peter, from Mistletoe Farm, gave him all the help he could. Together they chose the best animals in the market, and bought pedigree hens and ducks, and a fine healthy sow.

His brother sold him ewes about to lamb, and there came a day when at last Holly Farm seemed a real farm! Cows mooed in the meadow across the lane, sheep trotted over the grass, and the great sow stretched herself out in the pigsty in the yard.

"Have we *got* to have her there?" asked Mrs Longfield, wrinkling up her nose in disgust. "I'm sure I can smell pig-smell already."

"Well, you can't, Mother," said Roderick, earnestly.

"Pigs only smell when their sties are foul and dirty. Our sow has a tiled sty, and it's washed down every day. You'll never, never smell Martha."

"Martha?" said his mother, startled.

"Yes – I've called her that," said Roderick. "It suits her somehow. I like her."

The hens rushed about the yard all day long, clucking. The ducks, white Aylesburys, swam vigorously on the little pond off the yard. Every creature looked healthy and bonny, especially Martha the sow – and everything seemed to Melisande and her mother to be very very noisy indeed!

"Surely our ducks quack more loudly than any others?" groaned Mrs Longfield, early in the morning. "And *need* we keep that cock? He wakes me up regularly at dawn."

"Yes. He's as good as an alarm clock," said her husband. "I get up as soon as I hear him. *You* needn't worry, Rose – you're always off to sleep again in a few seconds!"

The cows mooed, the sheep baaed. The stockman whistled, the door of the milkshed banged in the wind. Mrs Longfield complained all day long, and her husband tried to be as patient with her as he could.

"If you live on a farm, you must expect this kind of life," he said. "Cheer up, Rose – you'll soon be so used to it that you'll never hear the noises except as a sort of soothing background. And by the way, dear – now that one of the cows has calved, and we have plenty of milk, what about the butter? Pat, the stockman, says his wife can't do it any more, and to tell you the truth, I can't afford to have her either. It's easy to make butter. I'd like you to take on the job."

Rose stared at him in horror. "Make butter? I couldn't possibly! It's heavy work, swinging that churn over and over. I've watched Mrs Lacy, and I know I couldn't do it."

"Don't be silly, Rose," said her husband. "It's only a knack. You've hardly anything to do, and, you know, a farmer can't afford to have a wife who's idle. Most farmers' wives love to help. You must help too. And you must take on the chickens as well. I want you to feed them, collect the eggs, grade them and wash them for market."

"And clean out the henhouse three times a week too, I suppose?" said Rose, bitterly.

"No. I'll do that – or one of the boys," said her husband. "You know, you persuaded me to send Cyril back to school again, didn't you – or he could have done these jobs and many others. Do you want me to take him away after all?"

Rose resented all these jobs bitterly. She resented being told she had nothing to do. Didn't she do the dusting, make some of the beds with Ellen, do all the flowers, and most of the mending? What else did David expect?

"I suppose he expects the same of me as Peter gets out of Linnie," she thought, angrily. "Why did I ever come here? There's Linnie washing and cooking and doing a hundred jobs on the farm and in the house, and David thinks I ought to do the same. And he'll go on thinking it as long as he has Linnie under his nose at Mistletoe Farm, bragging about her pickles, and jams, and fruit!"

Linnie never did brag or boast. She merely took it for granted that these things were her job, to be done well and lovingly for her husband and children, and she did them, and was happy in the doing. She would have given Rose plenty of advice and help if her sister-in-law had asked her – but Rose would never ask anyone for advice!

With a very bad grace Rose took on a few jobs. She said she couldn't possibly carry the heavy chicken pails of food to the chickens and ducks in the morning, so Cyril offered to do it. It meant that he had to run to catch his bus every

69

day, and sometimes missed half his breakfast – but his mother, lying in bed with her own breakfast, didn't even know that.

The poultry had to be fed again in the afternoon before darkness set in, but that was easy – merely corn that could be scattered. Rose did that all right – but once or twice she left it too late and all the hens had gone to roost.

Her husband came along and found her scattering corn in the hen yard, almost in the darkness. He felt annoyed.

"Rose! What's the good of that? The hens have gone to roost. They won't come out in the dark."

"Well, they can eat it early in the morning, then," said Rose.

"They won't. The rats will have had it long before then," said her husband. "We don't want to encourage *them*!"

"Rats!" said Rose, and shuddered. "Oh, are there rats about here? I don't think I shall be able to feed the chickens if there are."

In the end, Sally fed the chickens in the afternoon, and collected the eggs. And when Roddy came home from school he washed them and graded them. Rose said it spoilt her hands to keep them in water so long, these cold days.

"Well, I *like* doing it," said Roddy. "But it will mean I'm in late for tea each day, Mother. You tell Ellen to leave me mine on a tray."

So after that Roddy didn't go in to the dainty afternoon tea, but had it on a tray anywhere he liked. And it wasn't Ellen who got his tray ready, either – it was Sally, and she saw to it that Roderick got a first rate tea, fit for a hungry boy. His mother would have been most astonished if she had seen Roderick devouring ham sandwiches, hard boiled eggs and a great slices of kitchen cake every day at half-past five, after he had done his "egg-job" as he called it.

He liked doing jobs by himself – but nowadays he pretended that he had someone with him – a dog of his own. He talked to his imaginary dog all the time.

"Here's a fine egg, Tinker – as brown as an acorn almost. Down, sir, down – you'll break the egg. And here's another. Nice clean lot today, Tinker. We'll soon be done and then we'll see what's on our tray. Down, dog, down – you're as licky as Crackers! I'll give you a whole ham sandwich to yourself, you're such a good dog."

Nobody heard him except the sleepy hens and one of the stable cats. Sometimes Punch and Pouncer, the two farm dogs safely in their kennels for the night, caught a sound of his murmuring voice and pricked up their ears. But nobody ever disturbed Roderick and his pretend-dog, Tinker.

CHAPTER 12

What Happened One Saturday

One Saturday a dreadful thing happened. An Alsatian dog, half-wild, got into the field where the ewes were, and chased two of them round and round the field. The shepherd had gone off for the day to see his sick mother, and Mr Longfield was at the market. So it was only Roderick who saw what was happening.

He got a stick and ran shouting at the dog. It turned, leapt over the hedge and disappeared. But the damage had been done. Before an hour had gone by both the ewes had lambed – and one ewe was dead beside her two tiny lambs, and the other was alive, with one hardly-breathing lamb.

Roderick was so full of pity and horror that he didn't

know what to do. Where was the stockman? He was nowhere to be seen! Where was the odd-job man – miles away mending a fence somewhere probably. Cyril was playing in a football match.

He rushed off to find Melisande or his mother. But when he had blurted out his story of the dead sheep and the half-dead lamb belonging to the other ewe, his mother turned white.

"I think I'm going to faint," she said. "Oh, the poor things. No, no – don't ask me to come, Roderick. I couldn't, I couldn't."

Roddy left Melisande to see to his mother, and went flying off again, sick with fear. He must do something, he must! Those little twin lambs would die if he didn't do something – and the third lamb was hardly alive.

He bumped into Sally, coming home from her Saturday shopping. He clutched at her.

"Sally! Come quickly! What are we to do? An Alsatian chased the sheep – and now they've got lambs and one sheep's dead. Oh, Sally, what do we do to save the lambs?"

Sally was startled. Then she began to run at top speed down a path. "I'll be back!" she cried. "Don't you fret. I'm fetching somebody."

She disappeared round a hedge and then Roderick heard her shouting and yelling at the top of her voice.

"Sam Twigg! Hey, Sam Twigg! SAM TWIGG!"

"Twigg!" thought Roderick, and his heart lifted. "If only Twigg can come, it'll be all right."

And round the corner with Sally came the short bent figure of Sam Twigg the poacher, limping a little as usual, with Mr Potts, his golden spaniel at his heels.

"Where be they ewes?" he called. Roderick tore up to him. "Here – up in the field," he panted, and the three of them went together through the gate and into the big field.

"Bad enough to lose a fine ewe like that, let alone a little new lamb," muttered Twigg, as he stood looking down at the dead sheep. Her twin lambs were wriggling, and were alive – but the tiny lamb belonging to the other mother had died.

"Can we bottle-feed these?" asked Roderick, almost in tears.

"No," said Twigg. "They'm too small. Come too soon into the world they have. Drat that Alsatian. This isn't the first mischief he've done by a long way. Sally, girl, we'll try the old trick to save these younguns. I'll skin the little dead one, and wrap the two live ones in the dead skin. Then we'll see if the mammy of the dead one will take to them and feed them. It's their only chance."

Twigg was wonderfully deft and quick. In a trice, with Sally solemnly and sadly helping him, he skinned the dead lamb as if it were a rabbit.

The mother had sniffed at it many, many times, wondering why it did not move. Twigg went to the other two lambs, lying by their dead mother, and wrapped the skin of the dead one right over them.

Roderick watched in wonder and astonishment. Whatever was Twigg doing?

But Twigg knew what he was doing all right. He carried the two wriggling new-born lambs to the mother of the dead one, and laid them down beside her, holding the skin tightly over them.

The mother turned away. They were not her lambs. But soon she caught the smell of the skin that lay over the lambs. It had the smell of her own lamb!

She turned her head round and sniffed. She sniffed again. Yes, that was the smell of her own lamb – and yet there was another smell with it too, that wasn't her lamb at all.

She sniffed more closely. One of the tiny creatures wriggled against her, and nuzzled into her soft wool. The ewe bleated very softly. "Ba-aaa!"

"She've taken to them," said Twigg, in delight. "See that? She's licking them now. Another minute and she'll have them for good. You watch."

Holding their breath, Sally and Roderick watched. The big ewe was nuzzling the little lambs lovingly. Carefully Twigg pulled away the skin, so that she could smell the two lambs more strongly. Soon their smell and the smell of the skin were so intermingled that the ewe could not tell one from the other. She didn't even notice when Twigg pulled the skin away and put it into one of his baggy pockets.

They watched the ewe with the two lambs. "She've taken them for hers," said Twigg. "Well, Master Roderick, it's a sad business this – and I'm right down sorry for your Pa – but at least we've saved him two of his lambs."

"Oh Twigg – thank you," said Roderick. "What do we do now? Anything?"

"When's Shepherd coming back?" said Twigg. "He'll need to put hurdles round this ewe and her lambs. I'll wait for him, Master Roderick. You go on in with Sally. I'll give Shepherd a hand with the dead ewe too. Don't you fret. Farming's a toss-up, always was. Got to take the rough with the smooth, though there's some as gets more of the rough than they deserve."

Roderick was quite glad to go into the warm kitchen with Sally. Ellen pounced on her at once. "And where have you been all this time, Miss, I'd like to know. The bus has been and gone this hour since."

"Ellen, it's not Sally's fault," said Roderick. "There's been an – an accident with the sheep. Sally's been helping me."

Sally took not the slightest notice of Ellen. She might not have been there at all. She went to the larder and got a hunk of bread and a bit of cheese and a glass of milk. She set them on a tray and spoke to Roderick.

"You set to and get those down, Master Roddy. You've

seen bad things this morning and you're upset-like. You get those down you and you'll feel better."

Roddy did feel better after he had eaten and drunk. He wondered if his father was back yet. He thought he had heard the car. He went out to see.

Yes – it was his father. Roderick wished he hadn't got to tell him the bad news. But then he saw Twigg going up to him. Thank goodness Twigg would tell him.

Mr Longfield looked grim and shocked. It was a serious thing to lose a valuable ewe and a lamb in such a way. Twigg pointed to Roddy, and then beckoned him.

"Roddy," said his father. "This is an awful thing for you to have been mixed up in. But Twigg tells me you were a great help, and you did all you could between you. Thanks, Roddy."

He went off to the field to see the ewe and the twin lambs, and to mourn over his dead ewe too. This really was a bit of bad luck. He had only had the ewe a few weeks too. He built a hurdle round the live ewe and the two lambs she was now very pleased with.

"Why didn't you tell your mother?" he asked, when he had finished. "She would have come and helped."

"I did tell her," said Roderick, turning away. "She said she felt faint. She couldn't come."

"I see," said his father, and then the two of them looked at one another. They didn't say any more, but each was thinking the same thing.

"Sally didn't faint. Sally's only seventeen, but she came and helped." And Mr Longfield was ashamed of his wife, and alas, Roddy was ashamed of his mother.

Mrs Longfield was amazed when she heard what Twigg had done to save the two new-born lambs. "That fellow Twigg!" she said. "That poacher fellow! I've forbidden Ellen to let him come to the back door. Fancy *him* doing all that."

"Rose – Twigg is no longer forbidden to come to the back door," said Mr Longfield. "You will please tell Ellen he is to have a cup of tea whenever he's round this way."

"But she'll leave if she has to give tea to all the poachers in the district!" cried Rose.

"Let her," said her husband and went out of the room. He actually banged the door. Melisande and her mother looked at one another.

"Oh dear – I do hope Daddy isn't going to lose all his nice manners now he's a farmer," sighed Mrs Longfield. "He's never slammed a door like that before."

"He's upset about the ewe," said Melisande. "It *is* a loss, you know, Mother. Perhaps we'd better not have that party."

But before they could say any more, the door opened and Ellen came in with a message. Then she went out again. Melisande looked at her mother.

"You didn't give her Daddy's message," she said. "About Twigg. Aren't you going to?"

"No, I'm not," said her mother. "What good is Twigg to us? Ellen's worth more to us than Twigg! We'd be lost without her. Daddy can have his way in some things – but *we* must have our way sometimes, too, Melisande, mustn't we?"

And Melisande nodded her head. *She* wouldn't give the message to Ellen either. Twigg should still be forbidden to come to the back door – nasty little poacher! What would it matter anyway?

But it did matter. Melisande and her mother had ranged themselves against her father – they were disloyal to him. The family was splitting up into ones and twos. It was no longer united as the Mistletoe Farm family was.

Meantime, because of Twigg, the ewe up in the field was happy, and two motherless lambs had a mother. And

Roderick was talking to his pretend-dog, Tinker, as usual.

"It was marvellous, Tinker. It's a pity you weren't really there. You should just have seen what Sally and I and Twigg did. It was like a miracle!"

CHAPTER 13

Of Gypsies And Other Things

The next thing that happened was the coming of the gypsies. One day the bit of common away on the nearby hill showed nothing but gorse bushes with a little golden blossom flaming here and there – and the next there were gaily-coloured caravans – three of them.

"There are caravans on the common, Dad," said Cyril. He had seen them from his bedroom window as he dressed. His mother looked from the sitting room window saw them too. They looked very gay and picturesque that fine morning.

"How pretty they look!" said his mother. "Quite a picture!"

"Dad won't like them," said Roddy. It was a Sunday morning, and the children were not at school. Roddy was preparing to walk round the farm with his father. It was small enough to walk round – though Mistletoe Farm had to be ridden round, it was so much larger.

Mr Longfield was certainly not at all pleased to see the gypsies. "This means we shall have to keep a watch on the hens and the ducks," he said. "Rose, give orders to the kitchen that any gypsy coming to the back door must be sent away at once and warned of the dogs."

"We shall get muddled soon," said Melisande, pertly. "We have to welcome Twigg – and warn off the gypsies."

"Melisande, I don't like that kind of pert talk," said her father, shortly. Melisande looked at her mother and slightly shrugged her shoulders. Really, Daddy was getting quite bad-tempered lately!

He wasn't – but he was already a little worried about the farm. The loss of the ewe was hard – and in the many little ways that he had expected to make ready money to help to keep the ordinary expenses of the farm down, very little was coming in. The butter was not being made properly. The hens were not laying well – and surely they were using far far too many eggs in the house? Mr Longfield had expected to sell double the amount he was able to.

He hated to talk over these things with Rose. She was impatient of such details – but surely, surely she could at least see to the butter-making?

The spotless dairy was no longer spotless. Where before the farmers' wives had put out their big bowls of cream to set for skimming, there were none. The butter-churn was hated, and Rose only went to see if she could make the butter when she had to have some for the house!

And now the thieving gypsies had come! Mr Longfield had been warned of them by his brother over at Mistletoe Farm. They slid into the farmyard at night and stole hens and ducks and eggs. They threw doped meat to the dogs to quieten them. They would even milk the cows at night in the field if they could get them to stand.

"All barns and outhouses are to be kept locked at night whilst the gypsies are camped near," Mr Longfield told Pat the stockman, and George the odd-job man. They nodded. They were good men and knew their jobs on the farm. They liked the trim little farm too – but they didn't like the "Folks up at the house." Particularly Ellen. Ellen looked down on them, and would not let them even enter her kitchen.

"Smelly fellows!" she said to Sally, her nose in the air. "And just look at their boots – do they never clean them?"

As George was Sally's uncle, this was a silly thing to say. Sally flared up at once and there was a loud quarrel between the two of them. Mrs Longfield, sitting in her pretty room across the hall, heard it and frowned. Really, country life was more than she had bargained for. Sally oughtn't to answer back Ellen like that.

She spoke to Sally and Sally sulked. Sally was a first-class little worker, quick and clean and cheerful, and a good cook for her age. She was punctual in the mornings and never minded what she did. She felt sorry for her master when she saw how little Rose helped him.

Cream went sour in the dairy. There never seemed enough butter for the hungry household, let alone to take to sell at the market. There was no bottled fruit, home-made jam or pickles in the store cupboard to draw on, as there was in other farmhouses. That was nobody's fault, of course, because the Longfields had come so recently to Holly Farm.

Still, all this meant added expense, and loss of money. Sally saw it and it worried her straightforward country-mind. "A trim little farm like this ought to be selling two hundred eggs a week and more – and half its butter, with that cow in milk – and keeping itself grand!" she thought.

So one day she went to Mr Longfield, when she saw him gloomily looking at three bowls of sour milk in the dairy.

"If you like, sir, I'll manage the dairy for you," she said. "Miss Melisande could give me a hand on Saturdays. I can't bear to see good things wasted sir – I'll set the cream and make the butter gladly."

"You're a good girl, Sally," said Mr Longfield gratefully. Then he hesitated. "But what about your wages? I doubt if I can raise them any more. My wages bill is pretty big already."

"I'm not asking for a rise," said Sally. "You let me have a little cream to take to my mother, sir, and that's enough for me!"

So Sally took on the dairy. Mrs Longfield was really very relieved. Now she needn't mess about any more in that horrid cold place. The butter never *would* come for her anyway, however much she swung that churn!

It was marvellous how it came for Sally. She hummed as she made the butter in the diary, and emptied the skim milk for the little calf, and set the cream for the next lot of butter. "This is right good work," thought Sally, marvelling that her mistress hated it so much.

Melisande helped her the first Saturday, and then went no more to the dairy. Let that strong hefty Sally manage it all! She wasn't going to wear herself out with that churn. Sally didn't say anything, but she thought very little of Melisande.

Mr Longfield sometimes wondered what his wife did with her days. He often thought of busy, bustling, happy Linnie – her days were full enough. What a pity Rose wouldn't take a few lessons from Linnie on how to run a farmhouse and do the hundred and one jobs that went with a farm-life.

One day Mr Longfield thought he saw a gypsy woman slinking away from the back-door. He questioned his wife.

"Did you tell Ellen not to allow any gypsy round the farmhouse?" he asked.

"Yes, yes, yes," said Rose, crossly. "I'm always telling her things from you. Why?"

"Only because I thought I saw a gypsy woman round at the back," said her husband, and said no more.

The gypsy woman came often, especially at night when Sally had gone home. She could tell fortunes and Ellen was very silly about that kind of thing.

She would stand at the back door whilst the gypsy read

80

her hand and told her wonderful things about herself. She would let her into the scullery and watch her whilst she "read" the tea-leaves at the bottom of a cup. She would remember all her dreams and ask the gypsy to tell her what they meant.

Rose had told her not to let the gypsies come to the door, but Ellen disobeyed her in this. Soon the gypsy knew exactly where the larder was, where the store-cupboard was, and even where the keys of the different places were kept. That big one was the dairy key. That small one was the henhouse key.

Things began to disappear. Sally's tea-cloths went. Kitchen knives and forks disappeared. One or two plates were missing.

Sally asked Ellen about them. "Well, scullery things are *your* look-out," said Ellen. "You should keep your eye on them. If anyone knows where they are, you do!"

Sally flared up immediately. "Do you think I take them home?" she demanded.

Ellen didn't answer. She put on her "sourpuss" face and walked into the hall. But Sally followed her.

"If you start saying them kind of things to me, I'll give my notice in," she threatened. "I'll tell my aunt Dorcas too! She'll come over here and give you a piece of her mind!"

So Ellen didn't say any more. But when Rose asked her what in the world Sally was shouting about, she said in a few spiteful words.

"A few things are missing from the kitchen, Madam, and I was just telling Sally I couldn't have that – and she shouted at me."

"Oh dear," said Rose. "I do so hope Sally isn't taking things home. Do you think she is?"

"I wouldn't like to say, Madam," said Ellen primly, which made Rose feel quite certain that poor Sally was a pilferer.

She turned her thoughts to more pleasant things. Her birthday was coming nearer. She must send out the party invitations soon. She turned and spoke to Ellen of the proposed party.

Ellen seemed quite pleased. It would be a change anyway – things were so dreadfully quiet in the country!

"The master says that we must try and make everything ourselves," said Rose with a sigh. "I suppose Sally can prepare a kind of cold supper or buffet, can she, Ellen?"

Ellen looked very doubtful. She didn't like that idea at all. It would mean that she would have to turn to and help in the preparing of the supper. "Well – I don't know, Madam," she said. "She's only a young country girl after all. You've been used to much better things than Sally can do – couldn't you persuade the master to let you have a load of ready-prepared dishes down from London? Like you used to, Madam. After all, it's your birthday."

Rose was weak. If Ellen said Sally couldn't do the meal, then Rose wasn't going to bother to find out if she could. She would order the things from London – so much easier – and oh, how much nicer they would be!

CHAPTER 14

The Days Go By

The invitations went out. Melisande herself wrote out the cards for her three cousins and for Richard Lawson and two of her own school friends. Cyril told her which of his friends to ask too.

"We're going to have a cold buffet in the dining room, and take up the carpet from the parquet floor in the other

room," said Melisande. "And dance there. We'll show everyone how these things ought to be done!"

"What about the food?" asked Cyril. Melisande was evasive about this. Rose had told her that she was ordering it from town by van – and Melisande had agreed to say nothing to her father. She decided to say nothing to Cyril either.

"Oh, we shall manage!" was all she said.

Roddy wasn't very thrilled about the party. "It's not the kind I like," he complained. "All this dancing business! I don't see anything in it. Susan and I would much rather have a proper sit-down meal, and games afterwards, like we do at Mistletoe Farm."

"We're not considering what you and Susan like," said Melisande. "You don't need to come if you don't want to. In fact, I'd rather you didn't. You always look such a mess."

"Is Richard coming on Lordly-One?" asked Roddy.

"Yes. It will be full-moon that night, so quite a lot of people are riding over," said Melisande. "Five, I think. What about you stabling their horses for them?"

"Well – I wouldn't mind doing that at all," said Roddy, pleased. "Yes, I'll stable the horses and look after them."

"I bet you'll be at the buffet all evening, gobbling away," said Cyril.

"I don't really know what a buffet is," said Roderick. "Is it what Mother used to have at her parties at Three Towers – a sort of long table loaded with all kinds of cold dishes – and you helped yourself, or asked for what you wanted? If it's that – well, I daresay I might visit it once or twice. I'm always so hungry nowadays."

"You shouldn't be!" said Melisande. "*I* saw the tray Sally got ready for you yesterday – supposed to be for your *tea* – sausage rolls and cheese and cake! I call that high tea – just like we used to have at Mistletoe Farm."

"That's why I like it," said Roderick. "I wish this farm was run like Mistletoe Farm. Our house is like an ordinary house, not like a farmhouse. Why, at Mistletoe Farm the hens used to look in at the kitchen door, and sometimes Dorcas would have a little lamb peeping in – one she used to bottle-feed – and she's often had baby chicks there. I'd like Holly Farm to be like that."

"Well, *I* wouldn't," said Melisande. "Go on out, Roderick – and do wash your face and hands before you come in again. You look as dirty as old Twigg."

"Ellen turned Twigg away from the kitchen door last week," said Roderick, remembering. "And this week too. He told me. He said she looked at him as if he was a worm she'd like to cut in half. He said he'd pay her out someday."

"Ellen can look after herself," said Melisande. "She's not afraid of old poachers! I bet Twigg helps himself to eggs if nobody's about near the henhouse!"

"That's a beastly thing to say!" said Roderick, amazed. "What's the matter with this family now? There's no kindness in it!"

He stamped out, holding out his hand to an imaginary Tinker to lick. Tinker was really a great comfort to him. He even slept on his bed at night. Roddy told Tinker everything, and by now his pretend-dog was almost real.

Roderick had settled down at Holly Farm now but he wasn't very happy. His father always looked worried. His mother still treated him as a rather silly little baby boy, when she wasn't being cross with him. Cyril took no notice of him, and Melisande had gone back to being snappy and high-and-mighty – a bit like Ellen, he thought. They hardly saw the Mistletoe Farm folk now, which disappointed Roddy very much.

"After all, we're not so *very* far away," thought Roddy. "But except for seeing Jane and Susan in the bus, and Jack at school, I never see anybody from there. I keep asking Mother if I can go over, but she always find some excuse to keep me away."

The Mistletoe Farm folk were being cautious about asking the Holly Farm folk over. Linnie knew that Rose didn't want to come, and she was sorry that Melisande now looked down on the happy home she had had at Mistletoe Farm. Holly Farm with all its little luxuries had turned her head. "And she had grown to be such a nice, sensible girl," thought her aunt, sadly. "Well, well – she hadn't learnt her lesson quite long enough, I suppose."

Susan would very much have liked to have Roddy over as often as possible. He and she thought the same about so many things – about Boodi, for instance and Crackers, and about young chicks just out of the egg, and skippitty lambs.

Susan, in fact, was the only one who went over to Holly Farm at all. She rode there on Boodi, and was always hailed with delight by Roderick. Crackers fell on him and licked him till his hands, knees and face were dripping wet.

Susan never went to say how-do-you-do to her Aunt Rose. She avoided Cyril and Melisande. "You see, they don't *really* want to see me," she explained to Roddy. "We should only just say something polite to one another, and that's all. So it would really be a waste of time to bother. After all, it's you I've come to see."

Roderick told Susan about his imaginary dog Tinker. He told her carefully, rather fearful that she might laugh at him. But she didn't. She listened, her face solemn and serious. She seemed to think that Tinker was as real as Roddy thought him.

"Where is he now?" she asked, looking round.

"He's lying on my feet," said Roddy. "And if you hold your hand out, he'll lick it."

"Susan rode there on Boodi."

Susan promptly held out her hand. "Yes," she said. "He's licking it. Oh dear – now Crackers is licking it too. Do you suppose Tinker and Crackers will be friends, Roddy?"

And, strangely enough, Crackers suddenly got up and began to roll about on the ground and bark and behave altogether quite madly. "There you are!" said Susan. "He's playing with your Tinker!"

Except when Susan came over on Boodi, Roderick was a very lonely little boy. No boys of his own age lived near. Cyril and Melisande thought him a baby. He liked Punch and Pouncer but they were too staid and serious to play with.

"They're so grown-up," he said to Susan. "They look at me as if I was a puppy, and they never want to play, like Crackers does. Anyway they're always with Daddy or Pat or George."

"The only *satisfactory* dog to have is a dog of your own," said Susan, patting Crackers, and fondling his drooping ears. "You'll have to make do with Tinker till you get a real one. Isn't Twigg ever going to give you one?"

"Yes," said Roddy. "He told me last week that Tommy Lane's spaniel's got a litter of pups now, and they're beautiful. He says I can choose one when they're old enough to leave their mother."

"You *are* lucky!" said Susan. "How did you get your mother to say you could have one?"

Roddy looked gloomy. "I keep mentioning puppies and how I'd like one," he said, "but Mother simply takes no notice. I'm going to ask Daddy straight out – no hinting like I have to do with Mother."

"I shouldn't like a mother you have to hint things at," said Susan. "I like one you can say things straight out to."

"Oh well – I suppose all mothers are different," said Roddy, loyally, though secretly he agreed with Susan. It really was a nuisance to have to keep hinting about a dog, instead of asking plainly.

The invitations to the party were all sent off. The replies soon came back. Everyone seemed delighted to come. Richard sent a very nice note, and so did his mother. Richard added a P.S.

"Coming on Lordly-One, specially to show you how beautiful he still is!"

Melisande laughed and thought of the lovely new frilly frock her mother had promised her. It was to be quite a long one, almost to her ankles.

"If only you weren't so *fat* still, Melisande!" her mother said. "Those eight months at Mistletoe Farm didn't do you any good in that way – another few months and you'd have turned in a country clod like Jane – or Sally!"

Melisande hated to hear her mother say she was fat. She looked at herself in the glass. Certainly her face was now plump and well-rounded, and her body had grown so that not one of her last winter's dresses fitted her at all.

"I don't think I'm *too* bad, Mother," she said. "I'm not half as fat as some of the girls at school."

"I should hope not," said her mother. "Big shapeless lumps most of them are! I wish you'd slim down a bit – and I wish your face wasn't so plump. I'd like you to take after *me*, not your father, Melisande. I've always been slim and I can't ever recall having a fat face."

"Oh well," said Melisande, "you'll just have to put up with me as I am, Mother. Anyway, I do look a bit better than Jane!"

"Oh *Jane!*" said her mother, with scorn in her voice. "I'm surprised she's even been able to stop biting her nails. I don't believe that child *ever* washes her neck! I only hope she'll turn up looking decent at the party."

"It'll soon be here!" said Melisande, with excitement in her voice. "Oh Mother – I *am* so looking forward to it. It'll be the greatest success that ever was!"

CHAPTER 15

A Little Plain Speaking

A week or two went by. It was February, a bright clear February with quite a bit of warmth in the sunshine that flooded Holly Farm and Mistletoe Farm each day. At each farm the ewes had their lambs and the air was full of the baaing of the mothers and maa-aa-aaing of the frisky little lambs. Susan and Roderick loved to watch them skipping about, their long tails wriggling.

On the hedges wriggled the catkins of the hazels, and Roddy thought "lambs" tails was really a very good name for them. A few more blossoms were out on the gorse, though it would not blaze with rich yellow until April. The birds were singing madly everywhere.

Susan's father, at Mistletoe Farm, was happy. He loved the spring. There was a tremendous lot to do on the farm at that time, but it was worth it. Young calves, lambs, piglets, chicks, ducklings – all these came in the spring. Then there was the drilling and planting, the joy of seeing the first faint lines of green in the corn-fields. Then the tree-buds began to swell, the first early primroses could be looked for – oh, spring on the farm was a time to sing and whistle about!

Linnie was always busy then too. She saw to the bottle-fed lambs, feeding them with Dorcas in the kitchen. The calves had to be taught to drink milk from the big farm-pail. Piglets had to be seen to. Hens were laying eggs at top speed every day, and these had to be collected, washed and graded. Butter had to be made. Linnie took charge of all these things, and Susan and Jane helped her splendidly.

But Linnie did not force them to do too much. They had their jobs, and unless she had to she wouldn't make them do anything extra.

"You're right about that, Ma'am," said old Dorcas, approvingly. "It's bad to put old heads on young shoulders. That never did do any good that I can see. Children have got to be children before they're men and women. They must walk before they can run."

"You and your sayings!" said Linnie, laughing. "I'm sure that long before you were Susan's age you could practically run a dairy, a kitchen, and poultry on your own."

"Maybe I could," said Dorcas. "But that don't make it right for other children to do."

So Susan and Jane had plenty of time to themselves, once they had done their jobs. They went for long rides on Boodi and Merrylegs together, because they both loved the country round about. Crackers loped along behind, panting.

"Getting his fat down nicely," said Susan, looking down at him. "I put him on the bathroom scales last night, Jane, and he's lost three pounds since we've been taking him with us on our rides."

"Good gracious! He'll soon be as slim as Aunt Rose!" said Jane, and they both laughed.

"Daddy says Holly Farm isn't doing too well," said Susan. "Did you know?"

"No, I didn't. How did *you* know? Daddy wouldn't go and tell *you* that!" said Jane. "You're always hearing things you're not supposed to hear."

"I couldn't help it," said Susan. "I was playing snap with myself under the table, and they didn't know I was there. I crawled out immediately."

"It's a funny thing how often you're under the table or behind curtains or in the corner," said Jane. "If I want to say anything private to Mummy I always look everywhere round the room first to see if you're anywhere about."

"Well, you've only got to say "Are you there, Susan?" and I'll say yes, if I am," said Susan, quite hurt. "Anyway – it's a pity about Holly Farm, isn't it? What's happened, I wonder?"

It was true that Holly Farm was not doing as well as everyone had hoped. Bad luck comes to every farm sooner or later, of course – but it did seem as if Holly Farm was getting more than its fair share just at present.

A cow had fallen into a ditch and broken her leg. One of the horses was mysteriously ill and could not work. Two other cows hung their heads and would not eat. Martha the sow didn't seem happy, and David Longfield was afraid that when the piglets came they would be puny, and no good at all.

The tractor had broken down, and drilling and planting had been held up. When David had told his brother all this, the two men had looked at one another in dismay. "I'll give you all the help I can," said Peter Longfield at last. "But it's a busy time with me, as with you, David. You'll have to make out the best you can with what bit of help I can give. I'll come and see the two cows, anyway."

David Longfield hadn't told his wife Rose any of his troubles. She wasn't the kind of wife you could tell bad news to – only good news. She wasn't like Linnie, whose husband knew that bad, or good, she would always want to hear all the news – to rejoice at the good, and comfort him when it was bad.

The Holly Farm children didn't know of the bad things, either, though Roddy had noticed that the two cows didn't eat. He had noticed too that one of the horses wasn't at work. He liked the three horses on the farm, though he didn't know them very well yet. He liked the cows fairly well but he still wished they didn't have horns.

At Mistletoe Farm the farm and the house were one united whole. Linnie knew every cow, every horse, and so her husband declared, almost every sheep! She knew which fields were to be planted, and which were to be pasture. She kept her eye on everything, and belonged to the farm almost as much as to the house.

She took her share of the farm produce and used it or sold it or stored it. She pickled eggs, and bottled fruit, and had jars of delicious pickled onions on her shelves and pickled cabbage. Her sheets were scented with the lavender bushes that grew round the little courtyard near the goldfish pond. House and farm were all one, and Linnie and her husband shared them both together.

But at Holly Farm the farm and the house were two separate things. Only Roddy in the house knew of anything that went on in the farm, and Sally knew a little. The others knew nothing – not even the name of a cow, or what was planted in any field. A row of blue-purple cabbage would not mean jars of delicious pickled cabbage to Rose – and the lavender bushes would not make Melisande think of bags of lavender to be made in the late summer and stored in the linen cupboard.

Holly Farm, and the buying of it, had been such a slice of good luck to the Longfield family – or so it seemed to them at the time. But good luck has to be held on to, and encouraged and deserved, or it will slip away un-noticed. Now the Holly Farm luck had slipped away, and soon everyone would have to notice it! Mr Longfield had seen it already.

Things were not right at Holly Farm. Rose was not loyal to her husband. She was ignoring his wishes and doing things he would disapprove of. She was disapproving of him too!

"You always fall asleep at night, just as Peter does at Mistletoe Farm!" she complained. "And you're never in to tea at half-past four. And I do think you could remember to scrape your boots well before you come in. Ellen keeps complaining of the state of the hall."

"Let her!" said her husband, sitting down heavily. "All right, Rose, all right – I know I'm cross and touchy and tired. I get up so early, I feel sleepy long before you do at night. And as for coming in to tea at half-past four, that's ridiculous of you. Whoever heard of a farmer who had time for fiddling about with afternoon tea? Why don't we have a proper high-tea at six, like Linnie does? I'm in then, and hungry."

"You're forever talking about Linnie and her wonderful ways," said Rose, in a bitter voice. "She's nothing but a shapeless, red-faced farmer's wife."

"And aren't *you* a farmer's wife?" asked her husband. "Come, come, Rose – you were pleased to get here and have a home together again – or so you said. But you don't do a thing to help. Not a thing. And when a man's tired and comes in wanting a bite and a bit of comfort, all you say is – scrape my boots well when I come in! PAH!"

Rose stared at him, shocked. He so rarely talked like that to anyone – and he was talking to *her*! She dissolved into tears. But for once in a way her husband didn't put his arms round her and pet her like a spoilt child.

"You don't back me up, Rose," he said. "That's what's the matter here. We don't all pull together. How many times have I said those gypsies are to be kept away from the house – and yet George tells me he sees one or other of them at the back door two or three times a week? And how many times have I said old Twigg is to be made welcome – and now I hear he won't come near the place because of our high-and-mighty ways. It won't do."

Melisande and Cyril came in at this moment. They were horrified to find their mother in tears. They had heard their father's angry voice as they came down the hall, but they hadn't for one moment thought that it was with their mother he was so cross.

"Oh Melisande, oh Cyril!" wept their mother. "Daddy's so cross with me. I do my best, don't I! He wants me to be like your Aunt Linnie – and I'm so *different*!"

Her husband got up and walked out of the room. For the second time since they had come to Holly Farm he slammed the door. There was a startled silence after he had gone.

"Don't cry, Mother," said Melisande, putting her arms round the slender, elegant figure with its crown of shining hair. "Dad will get over it. He's always so cross lately, isn't he? He was even cross when I told him about my new party frock."

"And he's getting just like Uncle Peter over at Mistletoe Farm," said Cyril. "He yelled at me last night because I put the radio on to hear a concert – and he said he wanted to read. But actually he was asleep. It's all right, Mother. We're on your side. If Dad wants to turn us all into clods and stupid lumps we won't let him do it!"

He didn't want to, of course. All he wanted was a little help and comfort from a family he loved and longed to do his best for. He went up to his bedroom and sat down heavily in a chair.

He meant to think things out – but he didn't. He had been up since six o'clock that morning and he was tired out. In two minutes he was fast asleep – and Rose was going to be very cross indeed when she came up and found him there!

CHAPTER 16

The Day Of The Party At Last

The day of the party came at last. It was on a Saturday, so the three children were able to help in the preparations. Rose was at her most gracious, because it was her birthday.

Everyone gave her presents. Her husband gave her a beautiful little brooch which he could ill afford – but he had felt sorry for his outburst of temper a few nights before, and was now trying to make up for it. He kissed Rose and told her that instead of looking a year older she looked five years younger.

She was very pleased with that. She loved being fussed and made much of. She felt a little guilty when she remembered the pretty dresses she had bought for herself and Melisande – and all the good things that were being sent down from a London store by van. But still – it was her birthday and David would probably only scold a little!

The sun shone brightly. Everything seemed set for a very successful day. Over at Mistletoe Farm Jane and Susan were trying on new dresses too, and Jack was trying his best to slip away before his mother insisted on seeing if his new suit looked nice.

"*You* ought to have a new frock as well, Mummy," said Susan. "Whenever did you have a new one last? I simply can't remember. Before I was born, I should think!"

"You're about right, darling!" said her mother, laughing. "Well – I might have a new one this spring. Now do stand still while I alter this button. Fancy you going to an evening party."

"I'd rather go in my jodhpurs really," said Susan. "It

would be much more sensible, because Roddy and I are going to stable the horses of the people who ride over. Richard Lawson is coming on his horse Lordly-One."

"Susan! You are *not* going to stable horses in your new party frock!" said her mother, firmly. "You quite understand that, don't you? I don't care what Roddy says. He must do without your help."

Susan looked very gloomy. What a pity! That would have been the best part of the party, stabling the horses and seeing to them – and the cold supper, of course. Roddy had told her of the wonderful supper they were going to have.

"Smoked salmon! Lobster mayonnaise! Caviare sandwiches! All kinds of oddments with things on I don't know the names of – and trifles and jellies and éclairs and meringues! I shall have at least six éclairs, Sue. You can go for the meringues."

Susan told her mother of the list of delicious supper-things. Linnie stared in wonder. "But – I thought Sally and Ellen were doing all the food!" she said. "They can't possibly make things like that – good gracious, Sally's never made a meringue in her life. I doubt if she knows what it is!"

"Sounds to me as if they're getting everything from some outside shop or store," said Jane. "I bet they are! Melisande wouldn't tell me a thing about the party when I asked her. I bet it's all bought stuff."

"Don't keep saying 'I bet,' Jane," said her mother, thinking hard. She felt worried. Goodness, if Rose was ordering things like that, what kind of a bill would David have? Really, Rose was too bad.

Over at Holly Farm there was much excitement at that moment, because Melisande and her mother were also trying on dresses. Rose looked beautiful in hers. She couldn't resist going down and showing herself to her husband.

But when she got downstairs, she heard angry voices in the kitchen. Ellen and Sally were quarrelling again.

"I tell you, I left that pile of washing in that pail there," said Ellen's scolding voice. "And when I go to it this morning to get one of my aprons to iron out, it's gone! And what's more, my stockings are gone too, my best ones – *and* that blouse you admired so much the other day, Miss. Now just you tell me – how do things walk off by themselves?"

"If you mean – did I take them – well, you know as well as I do, I didn't," said Sally, in a shaking voice. "How do *I* know where they are? You're always hinting that this is gone and that is gone. I never take nothing that isn't mine, and never have. And what's more, if you repeat what you've said again, I'll walk out, Miss Sourpuss!"

"Oh, you bad, rude girl!" cried Ellen, beside herself with rage. "Calling me names now, are you? Well, let me tell you this – I wouldn't be surprised if all those missing things are in your chest of drawers at home this very minute!"

Mrs Longfield walked into the kitchen, a startling vision in her new party dress. It was pale blue and had little sequins all over it. Ellen and Sally stared at her in surprise.

"Now Ellen," said Mrs Longfield, "don't quarrel like this, please. There's so much to be done on a party day. Sally, get on with your work."

"I'm going, Ma'am," said Sally, sullenly. "I can't work with anyone that calls me a thief."

"Oh Sally! You can't walk out like this on the day of a party!" cried Mrs Longfield, her heart sinking. "You must give me proper notice, anyway."

"I'll refund you my last week's wages, Mam, but I won't stop with Ellen," said Sally. "Unless you tell *her* to go. Then I'll stop."

"Very well, *I'll* go!" said Ellen looking very white and angry. Mrs Longfield could have cried. She took Ellen's arm.

"Ellen, Ellen – you know we can't do without you!" she said. "Or without Sally either."

97

"Madam – I tell you straight – things have been stolen – my things and your thngs," said Ellen, in a trembling voice. "And I stick by what I've said. It's more likely Sally took them than anyone else. Who else *is* there to take them, anyway!"

A knock came at the back door at this moment, and someone outside gave it a push. Twigg's brown, leathery face looked in. He looked surprised when he saw Mrs Longfield in her party dress, and the angry Ellen and Sally.

"Beg pardon," he said. "I just came to ask if Master Roderick was anywheres around. Been looking for him everywhere!"

An idea flashed into Mrs Longfield's mind. Twigg! Of course, *Twigg* might have taken the things! He was a wicked old poacher, everyone knew that – and if he poached and stole hares and pheasants and trout, he'd steal household things too. It wasn't Sally – it must be Twigg!

"Twigg! You've been told not to come to the house at all!" she called angrily. "How dare you disobey my orders?"

"Because them's not the master's orders," said Twigg, contemptuously. "Where there's a master I don't take no notice of what the missus says. I don't do no harm anyways."

"Were you hanging about last night?" demanded Mrs Longfield. "Did you come sneaking in at the back door then?"

"No, that I didn't," said Twigg. "I were up with old Tommy Lane. And for why do you ask, Mam? You thinking I sneaked in here and took your best silver away? For shame on you!"

His scornful voice and the words he said roused Mrs Longfield to rage. She said things she should never have said.

"You didn't take the best silver – but you look other things, didn't you, Twigg? You sneaked this and that –

whatever you could find. I've a good mind to turn you over to the police."

"If so be Mester Longfield wants to do that to me, well Mester Longfield's welcome to," said Twigg. "But not you, Missus. And now I'll be going. Good day to you, Mam, good day to you all."

Sally was sobbing as Twigg went. She began gathering together the few things she kept at Holly Farm – an overall and one or two aprons.

"Don't go, Sally," said Mr Longfield, alarmed. "I'm sure it's Twigg who took anything that's missing."

"Oh Mam, you don't know any more than Ellen there if it was Twigg or me or anyone else," wept Sally. "You shouldn't ought to have said it was him, Mam. You didn't know who it was, and nor do I. Nor does Ellen for all she says it's me. And you shouldn't ought to fall foul of Sam Twigg. He's a good friend, but he's a bad enemy. Now nothing'll go right with the farm."

"Oh, don't be so silly, Sally," said Mrs Longfield, angry and desperate. "You've no right to leave in a hurry like this. Ellen, tell her to stay."

But Ellen was dumb. Ellen was sure Sally had taken her things, and she glared at her in hate. And Sally went, still sniffing. She bumped into Roderick outside the back door and he ran after her in surprise.

"Sally, Sally! What's the matter? What are you crying for?"

"You ask your Ma," sniffed Sally, and set off at top speed to her home a mile away.

Roderick went indoors to find his mother, feeling puzzled and anxious. She had gone, half-crying, to the sitting room, and Ellen had followed her.

"What's happened?" said Roddy, his head round the door.

"Nothing to do with you," said his mother. "Go and find your father and tell him I want him."

Roddy disappeared again, feeling suddenly gloomy.

"The gypsies fled with the dogs bounding after them."

Whatever could have happened? Where was his father? Up by the cowsheds, probably.

As he came near the sheds he saw a figure slinking round the corner. Who was it?

Then he heard a shout. It was his father. "Hey you – what are you doing here? I've turned you off my land six times already!"

Roddy ran to see who it was – surely, surely not old Twigg! No – of course not. It was a gypsy in a shawl, bright gold earrings swinging from her ears. Her bold black eyes stared brazenly at the farmer.

"I came to bring something to Miss Ellen, down at the farmhouse," said the gypsy in a lazy drawl. "I've got something for her. She said to come today."

"Don't lie," said the farmer. "You're forbidden the house, and you know it. Clear off!"

Another figure rose up out of the nearby hedge. It was a second gypsy, a man this time, a dirty-looking rogue who also had gold earrings in his ears.

"We ain't done no harm, Mister," he whined.

"What – another of you!" shouted the farmer in a rage. "I'll set the dogs on you! Hey, Punch, Pouncer – chase 'em off my land!"

The gypsies fled, with the dogs bounding after them. The man shook his fist and shouted out something Roddy couldn't hear.

"Will Punch and Pouncer bite them?" he asked, anxiously.

"Oh no – but they'll give them a good fright," said his father. "Your mother wants me, you say? All right. I'll come this very minute."

CHAPTER 17

From Bad To Worse

Roddy went with his father, feeling upset and worried. What with Sally and Ellen and his mother – and now the gypsies and the dogs – things were certainly getting rather worrying.

They left the cowsheds and went down towards the farmhouse. As they came near a van drew up at the gate. It had a name sprawled across the side. "Harridges, London."

"Now, what do *they* want?" said Mr Longfield. "Go and see, Roddy."

Roddy went. The man was unloading big trays on which were packed the most delicious-looking things. This must be the food for tonight! Roddy's eyes brightened. It certainly looked good. He ran back to his father.

"It's the food for thought," he said. "A whole vanful, Daddy! Shall we really eat all that?"

His father stopped as if he was suddenly struck by lightning. "A vanful of *food*! What on earth do you mean?"

Then he strode to the gate himself and called to the man. "Wait a minute. What's all this?"

The man looked surprised. "Snacks and so on ordered for a cold buffet here tonight, sir," he said. "I was told to deliver this morning."

Mr Longfield looked at the great trays of expensive looking food. He couldn't believe his eyes. Surely, *surely* Rose couldn't have ordered all this when he had expressly told her that everything must be made and cooked at home?

"Got the bill?" he asked, curtly. The man handed him an envelope. Mr Longfield tore it open.

It was for thirty-seven pounds!

Thirty-seven pounds! Food for a party. And he couldn't even buy himself a new water-trough for his cattle! Mr Longfield felt sick.

"I'm sorry," he said to the man. "Take it all back. My wife made a mistake. I can't possibly pay for all that food."

"But sir – I can't take it back," said the man, puzzled. "You see . . ."

"TAKE IT BACK!" shouted Mr Longfield. "I tell you I can't pay for it. Take it back and sell it to some other idiot. You can't sell it to me."

"Sorry, sir," said the man, and loaded the tray back into the van. He got in, backed the van, and drove off without another word. Roddy was terrified. Whatever was going to happen?

"You still there, Roddy?" said his father, and put his hand on the boy's shoulder. "I'm sorry about this, very sorry. But it was the only thing to be done."

"What about Mother? And the party? What will happen?" faltered Roddy feeling as if the world was turning suddenly upside down.

"We'll go and see," said his father, in a grim voice. He turned on his heel and strode off towards the front door. Roddy went too, half fearful.

His mother, Ellen, and now Melisande too, were all in the sitting room. His mother was still in tears, and Melisande was trying to comfort her.

"Oh, David!" she wept, as her husband came into the room. "Sally's gone. And Twigg's been to the back door and I'm sure he's been stealing things – and he said dreadful things to me – threatened he'd be our enemy, and. . . ."

"Rose," said her husband, not noticing Ellen was there, "did you order food from Harridges, after I'd said we were to have it all prepared at home?"

"Oh David – don't talk to me in that voice, *please*," sobbed Rose. "I can't bear it."

"Answer me, Rose," said her husband. He thrust a piece of paper at her. "Look – thirty-seven pounds for food for a party! Are you mad? It came in a van just now and I've sent it all back."

"Oh *Daddy*!" said Melisande, miserably.

"So you knew too, did you?" said her father, turning on her. "What sort of family have I got – paying no heed to my wishes, doing things behind my back – getting me in debt when I'm trying to make my way!"

He suddenly noticed Ellen was there. He turned on her too. "Yes, and I've got something to say to you too, Ellen! Those gypsies – they say you've been having them at the house – one was coming to bring you something this morning. How dare you disobey my orders?"

"What orders?" said Ellen, in fright. "I've disobeyed nobody. I. . . ."

"Pah!" said her master, in disgust. "You're all alike, the whole lot of you – can't be trusted in any way. I tell you this, Ellen – if you disobey my orders once more, you can go. I'm not having anybody I can't trust in *this* house. Now go to the kitchen. I want to talk to my wife without you glowering there."

Ellen fled out of the room and shut the door. She was trembling. What a terrible morning. And that party coming tonight – with no food prepared now – and no Sally to help!

She stood in the deserted kitchen for a minute or two, thinking. Then she ran upstairs quickly. Ellen wasn't staying to help with any party – no, not she. She'd teach the master to talk to her like that! She'd give them all the slip, catch the bus, and then the train – and go off to her sister's. She never did like a country life, anyway. Why, they'd expect her to churn the butter next, now Sally was gone. Let them do the jobs themselves!

Mr Longfield hadn't many more words to say. He was feeling sad and sick at heart. He spoke a little more kindly to the sobbing Rose.

"Do what you like about your party. If you like to call up Linnie, no doubt she'd bring over some food and help you out. But don't expect me to come and dance and make merry, Rose. It's not in my heart to be glad over anything today."

"You're cruel, you're unkind," wept Rose.

Her husband looked sadly at her. Then he noticed that she was wearing a new and beautiful frock – and so was Melisande too. His face hardened.

"I suppose you're going to present me with a bill for those frocks too?" he said bitterly. "Well, you can send them back. I've no money to pay for them. If you'd done what every farmer's wife likes to do, and made money out of your hens and your butter, you'd have had plenty to pay for your finery yourself, Rose. In future, it's no work, no pay, for both of us. We shall have to learn to go without nearly all the things we want!"

He went out – but this time he didn't slam the door, though he would have liked to. Slamming doors wasn't going to be any help now. If he didn't look out, he would be the cause of making his brother Peter lose money on the farm. If only those cows would pull round – and that horse. And if only the sow would have a litter of fine little piglets! If only – if only. . . . Yes, and if only Rose were like Linnie, somebody who pulled with him all the time, instead of against him. And there was Melisande going the same way too.

Inside the house Melisande and her mother were trying

to think what was best to do about the party. "We *must* make up our minds at once, Mother," Melisande kept saying to the distraught Rose. "We must, we must."

"For all this to happen on my birthday too!" wept Rose.

"Let's telephone to Aunt Linnie," said Roderick. "She always knows what to do."

"Yes. Mother, perhaps she would help us with the food – bring a lot over," said Melisande. "She's always got such a store. And Ellen would help, I'm sure she would. Oh, what a pity Sally's gone!"

"Go and ask Ellen if she'll help," said Rose, after they had discussed the whole thing for about twenty minutes, feeling more and more disconsolate.

Melisande went out into the kitchen. Ellen wasn't there. Melisande called her. "Ellen! Where are you?"

There was no answer. Melisande ran upstairs and knocked on Ellen's door. "Ellen, are you here? Mother wants to speak to you."

All was silence in the bedroom. Melisande knocked again and then opened the door. The bedroom looked very bare and tidy. No brush and comb on the dressing-table. No photographs of her sister on the mantelpiece. No nightdress case on the bed. In panic Melisande looked in the hanging cupboard. It was empty.

Ellen had gone – gone without a word, without even saying goodbye. Sally gone – Ellen gone. What a terrible, terrible day! Melisande ran downstairs and broke the news to the horrified Rose.

"But whatever shall we *do*?" said Rose, wringing her hands. "Both of them gone! Oh, we can't possibly have the party then. Ring your Aunt Linnie, Melisande and tell her what has happened. I shall be ill, I know I shall."

Melisande rang her aunt. Linnie listened, shocked. Melisande poured out everything – how her father had sent back the food – how cross he was about the dresses –

how he had spoken so sharply to Ellen that she had gone – oh, wasn't he unkind, and wasn't it all dreadful? On the day of the party too!

Linnie listened in silence. She saw at once what had happened. The house had been divided against itself – and as always happens, it couldn't stand. The household had collapsed, Ellen and Sally had deserted it – and now hard times were coming for Holly Farm.

"I'm sorry about all this, dear," Linnie said at last in her warm, clear voice. "You can't have the party of course. You must ring everyone up and put them off. Say your mother is not feeling very well. I am sure she can't be, with all these things happening. I'll be over tonight to see your mother and we must plan what we can do."

She rang off and went to find her husband. What a to-do! Would it break the little family at Holly Farm? Or make them? Linnie didn't know. It all depended on Rose – and Rose wasn't much of a staff to lean on!

Susan as usual heard what was said on the telephone. She was horrified. She ran to saddle Boodi. She would go over to Roddy at once. He might want a bit of help. She might even leave Crackers with him for the weekend if he wanted him. That was the very biggest piece of help she could think of!

CHAPTER 18

A Dreadful Day

It took Melisande a long time to ring up all the guests and cancel the party. By the time she had finished it was almost one o'clock. Her father came into the hall, dirty and tired.

"Anything for dinner?" he asked.

"Oh *dear*!" said Melisande. "Is it dinner-time. Perhaps Mother has got something ready. I've been simply ages on the phone."

She ran to see – but not even the cloth was spread on the table. She called loudly "Mother! Mother! Where are you? What about dinner?"

A voice answered her from the kitchen. "I'm here, Melisande. I simply can't find out where anything is. And there seems hardly any food in the house."

"Well, we meant to finish up all the bits tomorrow – what was left from the party," said Melisande. "And Sally would have cooked a chicken too, and made a pie. So naturally there won't be much in the larder now. Daddy wants his dinner. I'd better get it, if you can find something to put on the table."

"But where *is* everything?" said her mother, who had now changed out of her beautiful dress, and was in a morning one. "I can't even find a kitchen knife to do potatoes."

"Let's put them in the oven in their jackets then," said Melisande. "You scrub them, Mother."

"But where are the *potatoes*?" said Rose. She sounded quite helpless.

"They must be somewhere about," said Melisande. "Hello, here's Roddy. Roddy, do *you* know where anything is in this kitchen? Potatoes, for instance?"

"Oh yes," said Roddy, "they're in the outhouse off the scullery. I'll get some. I know where everything is. I come and poke about out here when Ellen's out. I say – has she really gone?"

"Yes," said Melisande. "And we shall be in a fine old mess now."

"Well, I'm glad she's gone," said Roddy. "Old Sourpuss! Now perhaps Sally will come back."

"Oh – I *wish* she would!" said Melisande, at once. "She's so sensible!"

It was quite incredible, but it took Melisande and her mother over an hour to get the meal. The potatoes took ages to do in their jackets, and finally they had to be taken out of the oven, cut open and mashed, or they would never have been ready. Rose opened a tin of cold meat and cut herself. It took five minutes to bandage her finger, and she sat down for another five minutes because the sight of blood upset her.

Melisande began to despair of ever getting the meal ready. Cyril banged in and out impatiently, but he didn't try to help. Roddy whistled aggravatingly all the time. Everyone was hungry and cross.

"If I don't get something to eat soon I shall have to go out without anything," said Mr Longfield, appearing in the kitchen. "For goodness sake – does it take an hour to get a bit of meat and potato and bread and cheese on the table?"

In the end he got a hunk of bread and cheese for himself and marched off angrily. What a household! But as soon as he was outside the house he forgot his household worries and thought about a whole lot of farm anxieties. He was glad that his brother was coming over that evening with Linnie. He could talk over his worries with him.

It really was a dreadful day. There were so many many things to be done that Ellen and Sally did easily and quickly, but which Melisande and her mother couldn't seem to tackle at all. Melisande was better than Rose because at least she had had to help a good bit when she stayed at Mistletoe Farm. But still it was like a nightmare – this to be done, and that, and then a dozen more things, and then oh dear, who was to make the butter?

"And there's the hens to feed – Sally always did that in the afternoons," said Melisande. "Roddy, will you do them? And do the eggs?"

"Of course. I always do the eggs anyway," said Roddy,

calmly? "Why can't Cyril do the butter? You've got heaps to do in the house."

So Cyril was turned firmly into the dairy and found out that butter wouldn't come any more quickly or easily for him than for his mother or Melisande!

Susan turned up on Boodi, of course, complete with a pile of sandwiches and slices of cake. "We'll picnic somewhere," she said to Roddy. "I expect Melisande and your mother will be glad not to have to bother about us for dinner this morning."

Roddy told Susan all about the upsets of the morning. "And when Twigg came, Mother accused him of stealing the missing things," he said. "So now Twigg's an enemy instead of a friend. Maybe he'll put spells on our horses and cows and they'll die."

"Twigg wouldn't. He likes animals too much," said Susan. "But I don't expect he'll come to help you any more. And I don't expect he'll give you that spaniel puppy now, Roddy."

"No. I thought of that," said Roddy, gloomily. "I shall have to make do with Tinker. He turned and patted his imaginary dog and then patted Crackers.

Susan was really a great help. She cleaned the hen-house with Roddy, and helped to mend a gap in the wire. She took the calf its pail of skim milk and let it drink. She saw that Pouncer was limping and turned up his paw and took out a thorn. In fact, she was her usual, sensible self, and Roddy felt a great deal better after about two hours of her company.

"Mummy said I could stay with you till she comes over this evening," said Susan. "You can have a ride on Boodi if you like. But I warn you, he's not very good today. He might rub your leg against the hedge, or something."

"I'll watch out," said Roddy and mounted the barrel-like pony. Sure enough, Boodi played his tricks that

110

afternoon, but Roddy was more than a match for him. As soon as Boodi pressed near the hedge to squeeze Roddy's leg against it, Roddy threw his leg over the saddle and yelled "Bad Boodi! Bad Boodi!"

"I do wish I had a pony of my own," said Roddy, regretfully, as he leapt down again. "But it seems that things are not going very well here – so I don't expect any of us will have ponies this year, anyway."

"Which would you rather have – a pony or a dog?" asked Susan, tickling Crackers.

"Oh, a *dog*," said Roddy, promptly.

"I thought perhaps I might have lent you Crackers over the weekend if you felt upself about things," said Susan. "But you don't seem too bad."

"I feel much better since you came," said Roddy. "I'd love to have him – but Mother would have a fit, and I couldn't make her more worried than she is."

"No. I suppose you couldn't," said Susan, very glad that she hadn't got to leave Crackers behind after all. "Who's going to do all the housework and cooking, Roddy, now that Ellen and Sally have both gone?"

"I don't know. Somebody, I suppose," said Roddy, vaguely. "Perhaps your mother would lend us Dorcas."

"She jolly well wouldn't!" said Susan, with a snort. "Why should she? It won't do your mother or Melisande any harm to do their own work for a bit."

"But they don't know how to," said Roddy. "I could clean the boots and shoes, I suppose," he said hopefully. "I like doing that sort of thing. I could do them before I go to bed. And I could bring in the logs for the fires and the coal for the kitchen."

"Aunt Rose won't enjoy washing up and scrubbing the kitchen floor and getting meals, will she?" said Susan, a little maliciously. Roddy said nothing. He found himself wishing that his mother was more like Susan's mother. His

111

"Bad Boodi! Bad Boodi!"

Aunt Linnie wouldn't groan and moan and sit around in tears, and say what a pity all this had happened on her birthday – she would know exactly what to do and set to work to do it. So would Jane. Would Melisande? Perhaps.

What about Cyril? Would he do much to help? Cyril

112

had been rather silly, lately, Roddy considered – spouting poetry again, and going on about the wonderful music on the Third Programme. Roddy didn't care about the Third Programme. There was never anything funny or anything exciting on it at all, and he couldn't think why Cyril was always raving about it.

"Do you remember how your father used to shout at Cyril in the evenings, when he wanted to turn on the radio?" asked Roddy, remembering. "When we were all at Mistletoe Farm, I mean. Well, Daddy does it too now – he made me jump out of my skin the other night, he yelled at Cyril so. I must say I rather like Daddy when he yells."

"Yes, I do too," said Susan. She was just about to say that the person he ought to yell at most of all was her Aunt Rose, when she stopped herself in time. Roddy was always loyal to his mother, whatever fault he might find in her himself.

"What time is it?" asked Susan, when they had finished feeding the hens, collecting the eggs and washing them. "Goodness – quarter to five! I'm beginning to feel a bit hungry, aren't you? When do you have high tea?"

"We don't have it," said Roddy, gloomily. "We have a dreadful sort of dainty afternoon tea – all mats and cloths and things, with hardly anything to eat. Usually Sally lets me have a tray with something decent on it all to myself – but now she's gone I suppose I won't have it – unless I get it myself."

"Well, get it yourself then," said Susan. "Let's wait till we're a bit hungrier and we'll go and collect something out of the larder."

There was no afternoon tea that afternoon. Rose had gone to lie down at three o'clock, and had fallen fast asleep. Melisande was struggling with things in the dairy, doing her best to help Cyril. Neither of them had any idea of the time.

When they at last went to look at the clock in the kitchen

113

it said half-past five! "No wonder we're hungry!" said Melisande. "Goodness – wouldn't I like to tuck in at one of Aunt Linnie's high teas today!"

Her father came into the kitchen too, at that moment and heard what she said. "I agree with you," he said. "High tea at this time's just right on a farm – and my word, look here – there's your Aunt Linnie coming along with her hands full of food. Bless her! She knew we'd welcome something to eat over the weekend!"

And, before ten minutes was up, everyone except Rose, who was still dozing, was sitting round the table tucking into ham and sausage rolls and cheese and cake – and drinking scalding hot tea made the way Linnie always made it – better than anyone else, so everyone declared.

Rose came down, half asleep – and stared in silence at the party round the table, and the obvious high tea that was going on.

"Come on, Mother!" said Roddy, making room for her. "This is just as good as being back at Mistletoe Farm – everybody round the table, plenty of decent food to eat, and lots of talk going on!"

CHAPTER 19

Holly Farm In A Muddle

Linnie left a good deal of food at Holly Farm for the week-end – half a ham, an enormous cake that Dorcas had baked specially for them that afternoon, some jam tarts and a cold roast chicken.

Her brother-in-law, David, was grateful. He took her hand

in his and pressed it. "You're good and kind, Linnie. I'm afraid we're in for rather a bad time now – no help in the house, unless the stockman's wife can give a hand – and Rose isn't really capable of tackling things."

"Well, she must try, David," said Linnie. "I will give her any advice or help that I can, you know that. Your three children can help a lot too – they *had* to help when they lived with me!"

Sunday was a muddle, and Rose was in despair most of the day, when she realised all the things there were to do. Melisande began to feel rather impatient with her mother. Fancy taking twenty minutes to make one bed!

Cyril said he didn't mind helping on the farm, but he wasn't going to mess about the house. "You might at least help with the washing-up," said Melisande, crossly.

"*I'll* do that," said Roddy. "And look – I've cleaned all the boots and shoes. There they are on the scullery floor."

So *that's* what you've been doing all this time!" said Melisande. "I wondered where you were. Oh Roddy – you *have* done them nicely! It's such a horrid job too – cleaning shoes."

"I like it," said Roddy. "I'll do what I can to help you, Melisande, so long as it isn't things like making beds or dusting. You can give me things like *cleaning* to do. I wouldn't even mind scrubbing this scullery floor for you, like Sally used to do. I like making things clean."

"That's funny –seeing you always look such a little grub yourself!" said Melisande. "Mother – look how well Roddy's cleaned the shoes! Really, he's a great help isn't he?"

"Dear little Roddy!" said her mother, drifting into the scullery, looking harassed and pale. "I don't know what we should do without him. You want to help Mother all you can, don't you?"

Roddy didn't like it when his mother talked to him in this baby way. He nodded and went out.

"Funny, solemn boy!" said Mrs Longfield, looking vaguely round the scullery. "Oh Melisande – isn't this awful? I simply don't know where to begin, do you?"

"Daddy's gone to see if Mrs Johns, the stockman's wife, will come and give a bit of help," said Melisande. "I only hope she can! And Aunt Linnie is going to get Dorcas to ask Sally to come back, now Ellen's gone. But even if she does, we'll have to do most of the housework ourselves, Mother – and as I shall have to be at school all day, I don't know how you're going to manage!"

Tears came into Rose's eyes. Melisande looked at her in exasperation. Then she remembered how she herself had always been able to "turn on the tap" at any moment, as Jack used to call it, when they stayed at Mistletoe Farm. Still, she, Melisande, had grown out of it – Mother never had.

She took no notice of her mother's tears, and piled the breakfast things into the steaming water. She was thankful to have plenty of hot water. There was none at Mistletoe Farm. Every drop had to be boiled on the kitchen stove. Here, at Holly Farm she had only to turn the tap and out came the water, steaming hot.

Aunt Linnie telephoned during the day. "Is that you, Melisande? I've got bad news, I'm afraid, dear. Sally has just been in to see Dorcas – and she's already got herself another job and is starting tomorrow. What a pity!"

"Oh *dear*!" said Melisande, in despair. "Can't she possibly cancel that and come back here?"

There was a slight pause at the other end. "I don't think she wants to," said her aunt's voice. "It's this business about those missing things, Melisande. Ellen thought it was Sally who stole them – and apparently your mother accused old Twigg. Sally's as honest as the day, of course – and she says old Twigg wouldn't steal from any Longfield, whoever else he might steal from! If only we could find the real culprit and clear up this unpleasant business! Even so, I doubt it Sally would come back. She seems to have taken a real dislike to your mother."

Rose was amazed when Melisande repeated this conversation to her. "Sally doesn't like me – when I was so kind to her!" she kept repeating. "I suppose she adores your Aunt Linnie, though!"

Her husband came in, stamping the mud off his boots at the door. He called out to them. "Mrs Johns can give you one or two hours each day, that's all. But it's something!"

He went away, calling Roddy to come with him round the farm. Roddy clicked to his imaginary Tinker and followed his father, pleased. He liked this Sunday walk round the farm.

"I hate that Mrs Johns!" said Rose, taking up a tea-cloth to dry the breakfast things. "Surly and rude! She picks her teeth too."

"Oh Mother – what does that matter if she scrubs the floor well, and can cook a joint or something?" said Melisande. "Roddy likes her – and I've noticed that the people Roddy likes are usually all right."

"Roddy's only a baby," said her mother. "He likes the oddest people."

"Mother, Roddy's *not* a baby," said Melisande, thinking of the rows of cleaned boots and shoes, and the way Roddy had come to fetch the chicken food and mixed it and boiled it up that morning. "I do think you should stop thinking he is – he really doesn't like the baby way you speak to him sometimes."

"Melisande! Surely *you* are not going to turn against me too," said Rose, pathetically, and Melisande was sure that she would see tears in her eyes again if she looked at her mother. So she didn't look.

"Nobody's turned against you," she said, beginning to

sound impatient. "But Mother – couldn't you be a bit more like – well, like Aunt Linnie? She sort of holds the family together – and when bad things happen, they don't seem as bad as they are, because we all know Aunt Linnie's there to lean on."

Her mother threw down the tea cloth and went out of the room. *Linnie!* Everyone quoted Linnie to her! Linnie was the last person in the world she wanted to be like. Linnie was too good to be true – she knew how to do everything, she was a paragon of all the virtues! She was sure though, that Linnie never read a book, never listened to good music, never had a thought outside her eternal cooking and washing and her hens and butter.

"Well – I will *not* grow into a cabbage like Linnie!" said Rose, out loud. "I will *not!*"

Cyril, passing at that moment, heard her and was astonished.

"What did you say, Mother?" he asked. "What's all this about cabbages?"

"Everyone seems to expect me to behave like your Aunt Linnie!" said his mother, miserably. "And she's just a cabbage – or a – a turnip, Cyril. She's got absolutely no interests beyond her house and her horrible hens and their dreary eggs. I *can't* be like her! I must have music and poetry and books, and pretty clothes. Linnie's just a country clod."

"She's not, Mother," said Cyril. "You're quite wrong. She's as fond of poetry as I am. She *loves* good music too. Do you know, last summer when I got my radio (which by the way Aunt Linnie helped me to get) she used to come out into the old barn with me when there was a symphony concert on – and we'd listen to it together – with the hens clucking all round us!"

Rose looked at him in astonishment. He went on earnestly. "She knows far more poetry than I do – she

reads all she can, though she's hardly a minute to spare. But none of these things *show* because she puts her family and the farm first – that's all. But she's not a clod or a cabbage or a turnip – or anything you've called her! I bet she could be far cleverer than anyone in our family, if she had more time."

"You never told me this before, Cyril," said his mother. "Nobody ever tells me anything!"

"Well – I didn't think you'd be interested," said Cyril. "And I knew you didn't like Aunt Linnie. It's a pity you don't, Mother. She could really give you lots of advice now!"

Once more Rose turned away in angry annoyance, her pretty face sullen and frowning. She went upstairs and fiddled about, straightening this and that.

"I'd rather leave this place altogether than stay on like this – and have Linnie thrust down my throat by everyone, even my own children!" she thought. "I wonder if David would give it up. I'm not fitted for a farm life. I'll wait till things have settled down a bit and then I'll ask him. If he really loves me he'll give it up and we'll find a nice little house in a town."

She looked out of the window and saw Roddy solemnly marching along with his father. "What a funny little boy he is!" she thought. "I don't understand him. He never tells me anything he thinks. He just seems to lead his own life – quite one on his own. But he's a good little boy really. It's his birthday soon – I'll buy him a really nice present."

She watched the two of them pass into the yard, talking very earnestly together. "What *can* they be talking about?" she wondered. "Roddy never talks like that to *me*!"

Roddy was talking about something most important. In fact, at the moment, it was the thing that loomed

biggest in his life. He was actually talking about the spaniel pup that Twigg had offered to give him out of Tommy Lane's litter!

And his father was listening with interest and pleasure! Would he say yes? Would he say that Roddy *might* have a dog of his own?

CHAPTER 20

Roddy Has A Wonderful Afternoon

Roddy hadn't meant to say anything about the pup at all. It all happened in rather an odd way.

He was walking with his father, and Punch and Pouncer were running with them. Roddy, conscious of his imaginary dog Tinker, who went with him everywhere, of course, wondered if Tinker liked Punch and Pouncer.

He decided that Tinker didn't. Tinker was like Crackers – a dog that knew his own worth, and although he said good morning and wagged his tail to the other farm dogs, he kept to the house and family. Tinker was the same.

"Come to heel, Tinker," muttered Roddy, below his breath, and turned to see it Tinker had obeyed. He had, of course. He was a most obedient dog. Roddy forgot that he was with his father and bent down and patted him.

Mr Longfield was puzzled. What was Roddy doing, patting the air like that? Then, a few minutes later, he noticed that Roddy was holding out his hand as if he was giving it to a dog to lick.

"Roddy – what are you doing that for?" asked his

father. Roddy put his hand down and went very red. He said nothing.

"It's almost as if you've got a dog with you that I can't see," said his father, sounding puzzled. "A dog that keeps to your heels, and that you pat – and then he comes and jumps up at you, and you hold out your hand for him to lick. What's it all about?"

Roddy looked up at his father, delighted. "Oh Daddy – *you* can almost see him too then! That's Tinker – my imaginary dog. I've missed Crackers so much, you know. So now I've got Tinker."

Mr Longfield didn't know what to say. He thought hard. How much Roddy must have wanted a real dog, if he had created an imaginary one! But an imaginary dog was no good to anyone. Roddy must have a real dog, that was certain.

"We must see about getting you a real dog, Roddy," he said. "You can call him Tinker too. But he must be real."

Roddy gave a gasp. After all his hints and worries and wonderings about asking for a dog – here was his father saying straight out that he could have one!

He immediately poured out all that Twigg had suggested about a golden spaniel pup.

"One of Tommy Lane's," said Roddy, happily. "His golden spaniel has a lovely litter – and Twigg said I could choose one. He'd fix it with Tommy Lane. But oh, Dad – Mother's offended him – he's our enemy now, isn't he? She said he's stolen things from Holly Farm. He's never coming again – so it's no good going to Tommy Lane's about the pup. He wouldn't give me one."

"Twigg won't bear *you* any malice," said his father, sad and angry to hear again how Rose had sent away Twigg in such a manner. "He'll not come near us again, I don't doubt – but he won't hold all this against *you*, Roddy. He's a kindly fellow at heart. Go and see him today, if you like."

"I could catch the bus," said Roddy, eagerly. "I could take my dinner with me in a packet. I'd be back before it was time to feed the hens. Oh Daddy – I never, never thought you'd say yes so easily!"

He darted off to the kitchen. Nobody was there. He made himself some badly cut sandwiches of bread and ham and cut a piece of cake. He wrapped them up in paper and set off to catch the bus, his heart singing. There was no time to tell his mother where he was going. He mustn't miss the bus!

His father went to see the horse who was ill. The animal was pleased to see him. It wanted company, and it liked this big, burly farmer who stroked it and talked to it comfortingly. The vet, had been already and had shaken his head. "Not too good," he had said. "But we must just hope for the best. There's nothing more I can do."

Mr Longfield sensed that the horse wanted company. He decided to sit with him for an hour. He looked at his watch. If he did that he wouldn't be able to be in time for lunch – and Rose would be cross. So he did just what Roddy had done – went to get sandwiches. He too, got his own, so as not to bother his wife or Melisande. He called up the stairs to where he heard them at work in the bedrooms.

"I shan't be in for lunch. I'm taking sandwiches." And out he went to his big shire horse. Animals were funny things. They wanted something else beside food and shelter, work and rest. They wanted comfort sometimes, because when they felt ill, they were frightened, though they didn't know why. They wanted friendship – and they responded to love and understanding more than to anything else. Mr Longfield knew that. Well – if this big old horse wanted anything of that kind now that he was ill, he should have it!

Roddy was in the bus, wishing it would go as fast as an

aeroplane. His eyes shone. He forgot about his imaginary dog for the first time for weeks. He was thinking of the pup that he would have – that *perhaps* he would have, he thought, correcting himself. If only Twigg was still friendly to him!

He came to Twigg's cottage at about two o'clock, for he had had to walk a good way from the bus. He knocked at the door. A dog's bark sounded at once.

"Come in!" called Twigg's voice and Roddy opened the door. Twigg was sitting in a ramshackle old armchair, rocking himself to and fro, Mr Potts at his feet. The dog ran joyfully to Roddy and fawned on him, slobbering all over him.

"Well! Here's a welcome visitor, Mr Potts!" said Twigg, and he twinkled at Roddy. "Come you in, Master Roddy. And what have *you* come for this Sunday afternoon – to see me or to see Mr Potts?"

Roddy laughed, delighted that Twigg was still friendly to him. "Twigg, do you remember you said you'd ask Tommy Lane for a pup for me?" he said. "Well – Dad says I can have it, so I've come over. But Twigg – do you still feel like getting me a pup, after what happened yesterday? I'm very very sorry about that."

Twigg gave him a gentle punch in the chest. "That's got nought to do with you and me, son," he said. "Women and their tongues is one thing, you and me's another. I won't say aught against your mother to you – but I'll not be coming to Holly Farm again this long year. As for the pup, we'll go straight-along and have a look at he!"

Roddy could have thrown his arms round the dirty old poacher. It was a puzzle how a man could be so bad and yet so good – how he could do such wrong things and such kindly ones! Still, Roddy wasn't going to bother his head about that – all he wanted was to see his pup!

They went up to Tommy Lane's little cottage. Crocuses

123

bloomed, and one or two early daffodils, but Roddy never even noticed them. He could hear tiny little yaps coming from somewhere!

Tommy Lane had heard them coming and he opened the door. "Come you in!" he said. "Mebbe I know what you've come for, young sir!"

A lovely golden spaniel was lying in a pile of old rugs. With her were four tiny pups, nuzzling round and rolling in the rugs with yappy squeaks. Roddy knelt down beside the mother dog and fondled her, his eyes on the squirming yellow pups.

One crawled toward hm, and he felt a tiny tongue licking his hand. He lifted the puppy up gently. It was the tiniest, dearest little thing, its ears already beginning to droop beside its beautifully shaped head.

"Mr Lane! Twigg! Could I have this one?" he asked, beseechingly. "I like it best of all. It came over to me and licked me."

"You have he, then," said Tommy Lane, nodding his untidy old head, and winking at Twigg. "You have he, young master – and train he well. He'll follow like a shadow at your heels, same as Mr Potts with Sam Twigg. Ah – you can't beat they spaniels."

Roddy was too overjoyed to speak. He fondled the tiny puppy, while the big mother watched him out of her beautiful eyes.

He found his tongue at last. "Can I take him home with me today? Is he ready to leave his mother?"

"Yes, he's ready," said Tommy Lane. "The first pup went yesterday, and he's all right. Give him plenty of milk at first – and let him feel his teeth on something as soon as he wants to. Fine little dog he be."

A thought struck Roddy suddenly. "Oughtn't I to pay for him?" he said. "I've got some money in my money-box still – Christmas money."

124

"Mr Lane! Twigg! Could I have this one?"

"I reckon four of these pups will be paid for," said Tommy Lane, "so I can give away one for nothing if I wants to. You keep your money, young sir, and spend it on your new dog – he'll want a collar soon, and a lead – and mebbe you want to bring him up in luxury like, and give him a basket!"

"You're *kind*, Mr Lane," said Roddy, burying his nose in the silky coat of the tiny spaniel. He smelt nice. "Someday I hope I'll be able to do *you* a good turn!"

"Well – me and Sam Twigg owes the Longfields at Mistletoe Farm for a-many kindnesses," said Tommy Lane, scratching the mother spaniel's soft head. "This here pup is a bit in return, like."

Roddy was very happy. He sat in Tommy Lane's cottage and ate his sandwiches there, listening to the talk of the two old countrymen. He could have listened for hours. The talk was of badgers and owls and hares and pheasants and foxes and weasels and otters and moles – fascinating talk for a young boy to hear. What a wonderful afternoon! Sitting there with his new pup pressed into his neck, and listening to the country wisdom of the two old men was a memory that was to remain with Roddy for the rest of his life.

He got up reluctantly at last. "There's no bus," he said to Twigg. "Could you please tell me the best way to get back across the fields – without losing myself!"

Twigg twinkled at him. "Me and Tommy will take you part of the way," he said. "We'll tell you the rest. It's quite easy, really."

They took him part of the way and left him to walk the rest by himself. As they said, it was really quite easy. He walked in a dream, his puppy in his arms.

"Tinker!" he said. "You're real now! You aren't just a little imaginary dog – you're a real one. I can feel you, warm and soft. I can hear you. I can even smell you! You're my very own Tinker-dog, and you'll belong to me and nobody else for ever and ever."

126

CHAPTER 21

A Shock For Roddy

Poor Roddy! He was met by cross looks and hard words when at last he arrived home just before dark.

"You naughty boy! Where have you been? You didn't come in for lunch, and you weren't at Mistletoe Farm!" scolded his mother. "We telephoned to see."

"Didn't Daddy tell you where I'd gone?" asked Roddy, surprised.

"We haven't even *seen* Daddy," said Melisande, also cross. "I've had to feed the hens too, and collect the eggs – just when there's so much to be done."

"Oh gosh!" said Roddy, remembering suddenly that he had promised his father to be back in time. He had utterly and completely forgotten. "I'm sorry, Melisande. I really am."

"But where have you *been*?" said his mother. "And what's that you've got there, wrapped in your scarf?"

Roddy uncovered the spaniel puppy, who was now fast asleep. "Tommy Lane gave him to me," he said. "Isn't he beautiful?"

His mother stared at the puppy as if she couldn't believe her eyes. She was very angry indeed. "A *puppy* – when you know I won't have a dog in the house! You can take it back. I forbid you to have it – without even *asking* me, too!"

Roddy went white. "He's mine," he said. "And Daddy said I might have him. I asked him."

"What's the good of asking *Daddy*!" said his mother, her voice rising high. "*He's* not got to look after him, and clean up after him, and feed him! You're to take him back."

"I shall look after him myself," said Roddy. "And feed him and everything."

"And what about when you're at school all day?" said his mother. "How can you look after him then?"

Roddy hadn't thought of that. All his happiness went. The pupy woke up at the moment and yawned a little spaniel yawn. Roddy set him gently down on the floor. Here was a perfect little picture.

"Look, Mother," said Roddy. "He's such a darling. Don't you like him now you see him properly?"

"Horrid little thing!" said Rose, obstinately. "Here's your father. I shall tell him you're to take it back."

But Roddy's father said no – Roddy could keep the pup, and the boy's heart lifted. But it sank again when his mother spoke bitterly.

Well, *I* shan't look after it when Roddy's at school!" said Rose. "If you think I'm going to bother to feed it and clean up after it, and have it under my feet all the time, I'm not. If *I've* got to train it, it won't enjoy its training!"

"You're cruel, Mother!" said Roddy, almost in tears. He could picture so well what might happen. His mother wouldn't give it food every few hours. She might smack it every time it got under her feet or made a puppy-mess. She would cow it and frighten it, and it would be unhappy. He looked at her with scornful dislike, and for a moment Rose was frightened at his look.

He picked up the tiny creature and wrapped it in his scarf again. He turned and went out, without heeding the calls of his father.

"I love you and you're my dog – but I'd rather you were someone else's dog and happy, than mine and miserable," said poor Roddy. He walked all the way back to Tommy Lane's, and opened the door. Nobody was there except the spaniel with her little family. Tommy wasn't back yet. He had probably gone poaching with Twigg!

Roddy put the puppy back gently on the pile of rugs. He felt in his pocket and took out a notebook. He scribbled a few words, and put the note on the table, where Tommy Lane found it a few hours later. Twigg read it to him, for Tommy couldn't read.

"I've brought back my pup. I mustn't have it, Mother says. But thank you, Mr Lane. Roddy."

He got back home about eight o'clock, tired and miserable. The family were anxiously waiting for him. They had put a meal ready for him on a tray, for they had had high tea long ago. It had been decided by everyone – except Rose – that high-tea would be more sensible now there was no one but themselves to get the meal. Rose could always get herself an afternoon tea if she liked to!

"Come here, Roddy," said his father, struck by the boy's tired and miserale face. "Where have you been? We've been worried about you? Where's the pup?"

"I took him back," said Roddy. "That's what Mother wanted, wasn't it? But – I don't think I'll ever be able to forgive you, Mother!"

He went out of the room and upstairs without touching the food set ready for him.

"How *unkind*!" said Rose, the easy tears coming. "Just because I objected to the dog. Why, Roddy looked at me as if he almost hated me then!"

"Do you wonder, Rose?" said her husband, wearily. "Hatred is so much easier to win than love – and so much harder to get rid of. Hadn't you better be careful?"

Roddy didn't say a word to anyone about the puppy he had had for such a short time. He didn't even have his imaginary dog any more. He got up as usual next morning and did his jobs well and thoroughly and caught the bus for school with Cyril and Melisande. But he didn't go and say goodbye to his mother – who, astonishingly enough, was still in bed! She complained of a bad night, and the others had left her to sleep.

"Though if she thinks Mrs Johns will get her her

breakfast when she comes, she'll be mistaken," said Melisande, tired already with getting the breakfast and making the beds before catching the bus. "Oh dear – I do so wish we had Sally. She was so sensible and nice."

Mrs Johns didn't take up Rose's breakfast. She had no intention of doing so. She banged about in the kitchen and scullery and woke up Rose completely. Rose rang the bell.

But Mrs Johns took no notice of bells. She just went on banging round. In the end Rose had to get up and get her own breakfast. Mrs Johns watched her grimly. She was a dour and surly woman.

"I've done round the kitchen and the scullery. Now I'm off," she said. Rose was dismayed.

"Oh, but I wanted you to do the other rooms too," she said, "and cook a joint for us."

"Ma'm, I've got my husband and six children to see to," said Mrs Johns, "to say naught of hens and ducks and goats and a pig. Think shame on yourself for lying in bed till this time of day, and not getting a bit ready for your man when he comes in. *I'm* not getting his dinner – I'm off to get dinner for the eight of us back home."

She banged her way out and slammed the door. Rose was angry and depressed. How dare Mrs Johns speak to her like that? But she wouldn't dare now to tick her off. If she did, Mrs Johns wouldn't come again – and then things would be worse than ever.

They were bad enough as it was. The next few days were uncomfortable and miserable for everyone. Rose didn't really try to cope with things, she felt much too sorry for herself. Melisande had to turn to before breakfast and do what she could – and after school she worked hard in the house and dairy too. Otherwise the house would have been a pigsty.

Roddy did his bit too. He didn't seem to mind what jobs

130

he took on. Melisande found that she was depending on him more and more. He *always* did what he said he would. Once, when Mrs Johns didn't come, he even scrubbed the scullery floor, which had got unbelievably filthy. He felt quite proud when he saw how nice it looked.

His father was worried about him. Roddy avoided his mother whenever he could and hardly spoke to her. He said very little to his father either. In fact, he looked a miserable, obstinate little boy, although he worked hard before and after school, and could be completely trusted with the hens and ducks and eggs.

One evening Linnie telephoned. "She wants to speak to you, Daddy," said Melisande, holding out the receiver to her father.

"David!" said Linnie's voice. "We've been thinking it might be a bit of help to you if we had Roddy to stay with us for a bit – till you get someone living in to help you. Susan would so love to have him."

Roddy's father turned from the telephone and spoke to Roddy. "Roddy – it's Aunt Linnie. She says they want you to go and stay with them. Would you like to go, old chap?"

Roddy's face lighted up. Misteltoe Farm – that place of warmth and friendship and love where he had been so happy! Aunt Linnie and her cheerful kindness – Dorcas in the kitchen – Jack and Jane to tease him – and dear old Susan and Crackers. Crackers! He could share him.

His father waited. "Well, Roddy? When would you like to go? Tomorrow?"

Then Roddy said a most surprising thing. "No, Daddy. Who'll do my jobs here if I go? It would be awfully hard for Melisande to have to do the things I do, as well as what she does now. Tell Aunt Linnie I'd *love* to come – oh, I really would – but I don't see how I can leave Holly Farm *now*."

131

His father gave him a long look. Then he turned to the telephone. "Linnie? He'd *love* to come – I can see he wants to with all his heart – but he's not deserting us, Linnie. He's standing by us!"

He clicked the receiver back into place. He went to the surprised Roddy and gave him a bear-like hug. "You've done me good!" he said. "Thanks, Roddy – I *do* want your help. You're a brick!"

He went out to make sure the henhouse and barns were locked. Such a lot of thieving had been going on. Melisande and Cyril, left in the sitting room with Roddy, looked at one another. They could guess what an effort it had been for him to say no to Aunt Linnie's offer. He did so love Mistletoe Farm – and Susan and Crackers!

"Thanks, Roddy," said Melisande. "As a matter of fact – *I* couldn't do without your help either!"

"You're a sport, Roddy," said Cyril. And for the first time that week Roddy beamed. His family wasn't so bad after all!

CHAPTER 22

An Enemy At Work

Three weeks somehow dragged along. Holly Farm was no longer a nice comfortable home to live in. It was dirty and untidy, meals were not good, and very often tempers were short.

Melisande had far too much to do, and she soon looked thin in the face, and lost some of her plumpness. She grew resentful because she thought that her mother, with all the day in front of her, seemed to achieve so little. She snapped at Rose, and Rose either snapped back or cried. Roddy and Cyril couldn't bear it. They cleared off out-of-doors as much as they could.

Mrs Johns still came in for two hours in the mornings, grim and surly, noisy as ever. Rose was so afraid of her that she never went near when Mrs Johns was in the kitchen. Which was a pity because the grim woman had a kind heart underneath her rough ways, and would have taught Rose many a useful tip.

Cyril found that suddenly he had a great deal to do on the farm. The odd-job man fell ill with a bad chill, and was away a week. When he came back he was not fit to do a full day's work, so when Cyril came home from school he had to turn to and do many jobs. He didn't grumble, but he didn't do them willingly, or in a friendly manner, which was a pity.

Roddy pegged away at his own jobs as usual, slow, but sure, and was always there when Melisande was in difficulties. If the clothes line broke he mended it. If the sink got blocked he miraculously unblocked it. If the boiler fire went out he could light it more quickly than anyone.

"Honestly, you're a marvel, Roddy," Melisande said, warmly. "You're more grown-up than any of us, sometimes! Roddy –listen – I *do* wish you'd had that puppy. I'm very sorry about that."

"I don't want to talk about it," said Roddy, and changed the subject abruptly.

Aunt Linnie came over twice with Dorcas. How Dorcas worked away in the kitchens, and how spotless and shining they looked when she left! How Aunt Linnie cooked and baked, and what a fine sight the larder was when she had done!

Rose hovered round, no help at all. Linnie spoke kindly but firmly to her.

"Rose – wouldn't you like me to show you how to do

some simple cooking and baking? There was hardly anything fit to eat in the larder when I came. Food is so important to a growing family – and what about poor David? He looks quite thin."

"I don't feel well," said Rose. "I'm hoping to get somebody in to look after the house. Then I can rest. I need rest. This is a very dreadful time for me."

Linnie sighed. As long as Rose thought only of herself, they would never get anywhere! She said no more, but was pleased to see Melisande's face when the girl came home and saw the full larder and shining kitchens.

"Oh *look* Mother! Isn't Aunt Linnie wonderful – and Dorcas too!" said Melisande, giving them both a hug. "It's the first time for weeks I've felt happy to come home."

"You've had some bad luck, no doubt about that," said Linnie. "It's time it went!"

But instead of going, it suddenly got worse! Roddy came flying indoors the next morning with very bad news.

"Dad! The ducks have gone – and half the hens!"

Everyone ran out to see. It was true. Only one solitary duck swam on the pond – and it was plain there were only half the usual number of hens.

"Who's done that?" said Cyril, angrily. "Who's been along and stolen them all?"

"It must be Twigg!" said his mother. "He said he'd be our enemy. It's Twigg!"

"It can't be," said her husband. "Twigg wouldn't do a mean thing like that to us."

"He would! He would!" said Rose. "He's not forgiven me for accusing him in front of Sally and Ellen of stealing those things!"

Mr Potts the policeman was sent for. He too was inclined to think it was Twigg. He pointed out some small footprints in the mud round the henhouse.

"*Everyone ran out to see . . . only one solitary duck
swam . . .*"

"Sam Twigg's got small feet," he said. "So has Tommy Lane."

Mr Potts had no love for Sam Twigg. Too often Twigg had met Mr Potts the policeman in the street, and had at once turned round and shouted to Mr Potts his spaniel – so that everyone imagined he was talking to the policeman.

"Hey, Mr Potts, come here, you! Potts by name and Potty by nature! Urrrrrr! Wicked Mr Potts!"

And the policeman had had to bear all the delighted winks and grins and chuckles that the village people gave when they heard Twigg's cheeky shouts. He was really very glad indeed to make Twigg the culprit in this business of stolen poultry.

"Well, I'll go and talk to Sam Twigg," he said, shutting his notebook. "Frighten the life out of him, I will. Ah, he's a slippery one that – but I'll get him some day."

And off he marched to give Twigg a most unpleasant half-hour indeed, and to make the old poacher very angry and resentful.

That afternoon the stockman had bad news too. He reported that about six of the cows were sick, besides the two already ill.

Mr Longfield hurried off to see them. As soon as he had examined them he telephoned the vet. This was serious. He was a very worried man indeed when the vet, came.

The vet examined the cows carefully. Then he stood up and looked gravely at Mr Longfield. "Have you any enemies about here, Mr Longfield? Someone's been doing something to damage these cows of yours – I can't tell you what, but something in the poisoning line."

Twigg's name came to Mr Longfield's lips but he did not say it. He could not bring himself to think that the old poacher would do a thing like this to him – even though Rose had mortally insulted him!

136

"Now that I've seen these cows I wouldn't be surprised if that horse of yours, and the other two cows, haven't been doped in the same way as these," he said. "See here, sir – see those little holes in this cow's neck? Well, something has been injected there – something that's made the cow sicken."

Mr Longfield felt sick himself. How could anyone do these things to helpless animals, just to revenge themselves on the owner? He turned at the sound of footsteps and saw Mr Potts the policeman again. He had come to report on his interview with Twigg.

"Afternoon, sir," said Mr Potts in a voice as ponderous as his walk. "About this here matter of Sam Twigg and your poultry, sir. I saw him and I saw Tommy Lane too. They were both out last night, but they both deny they were over this way. But you can't believe a word they say, sir."

"Who's this you're talking about? Twigg?" said the vet. He turned to Mr Longfield. "Well, Twigg *could* have done this all right, Mr Longfield, if he's an enemy of yours. He was in a racing-stable at one time, and he knew a lot about doping horses. I don't suppose he has forgotten his knowledge. He was always a twister, was Sam Twigg. Mind you, he's a marvel with animals. I admit it myself. Twigg can often do what I can't – but if he's your enemy, beware! He's a good friend – but I wouldn't like to have him for *my* enemy."

"There you are!" said Mr Potts, pleased with this long speech. "That's it, sir – Twigg was along here last night with old Tommy Lane – and the two of them took your ducks and hens, and worked mischief to your cows. No doubt about it, sir. I'll arrest him and put him in the cells – and Tommy Lane too!"

"What about the cows?" asked Mr Longfield, turning to the vet. "Will they live?"

"I doubt it," said the vet. "It's a big loss to you. They're fine cows, I know. Look, take these pills. Sit up with the cows tonight, and if any of them groan, give them these. It'll ease their pain, poor creatures."

He went over to where he had tied his horse, leapt on its back and rode off. "Poor Longfield!" he thought. "He's in a sad mess now. Those cows look like dying tonight. They're worse than the others were."

Mr Potts went off gleefully to Twigg's cottage again, pedalling away on his bicycle happily. Ah – now he'd got him, the old rogue, the pest, the toad! That was a very serious business – doping valuable cows like that.

Twigg listened, looking astounded. Tommy Lane was with him. Twigg took the policeman to a shed outside, lifted up some sacking, and showed the policeman four fine pheasants, still in their feathers.

"I *were* on Mester Longfield's land last night," said Twigg. "And them's what I got. But I weren't on Holly Farm land, I were on Mistletoe Farm land. And if you go and tell Mester Peter Longfield that, mebbe he'll send for me and dress me down hisself – but he won't go for to send me off to the cells with *you*, Mr Potts."

"You can't prove you got those pheasants on Mistletoe Farm," said the policeman, triumphantly. "I'll take you along to the police station for questioning, Sam Twigg. And you too, Tommy Lane. Come along, both of you!"

"I'll just get me coat," said Twigg, looking very subdued. He and Tommy went in at the back door of the cottage. The policeman bent over the pheasants, counted them, and made a few entries in his notebook about them. Then he stood up and called.

"Twigg! Lane! I'm waiting!"

There was no answer. All was quiet in the cottage. A sudden thought struck Mr Potts. He ran in at the back door and gazed round the tiny scullery. Then into the parlour. The cottage was empty!

"Drat him!" shouted Mr Potts, angrily. "He went in at the back – and out at the front. Just as I'd nicely got my hands on him too. I'll make him feel sorry for himself when I catch him!"

But it was difficult to know where he was going to catch Twigg. There wasn't a sign of him anywhere. In fact, it wasn't worth while bothering to look for him. Mr Potts knew that quite well. He went scowling back to the police-station. You wait, Twigg, that's all! You just wait!

CHAPTER 23

The Choice

That evening Linnie and her husband both went over to Holly Farm, deeply troubled. There seemed no end to the bad luck that had overtaken the farm. This last business of the cows was very serious indeed.

Cyril and Melisande were out in the dark dairy, lit by one small electric light, trying to churn the butter, which, as usual, refused to come till long after it should. Melisande was tired out. She had been up at half-past six that morning and had had a long day at school. Cyril too was tired. He had been up with his father at six, and out on the farm to help the odd-job man, who was still only doing half-time work.

They were cross and snappy. "I feel I'd almost sooner never eat butter again than have to get it like this," said Melisande. "Sally always got the butter to come much more quickly. We don't do it properly."

"Dorcas said butter came quicker for good tempered

people than for bad," said Cyril. "You temper's been so bad lately that no wonder the butter doesn't come."

"What about yours?" retorted Melisande. "Listen – is that someone's car I can hear? Yes – it must be Aunt Linnie and Uncle Peter. They're coming over for a serious talk to-night."

Roddy was in the kitchen, cleaning all the dirty boots and shoes again – and some of them were very dirty indeed, especially his father's and Cyril's. He had spread a news-paper on the floor so that he shouldn't make too much mess.

There was only Rose in the sitting room when Linnie and Peter went in. David was washing his hands, still worrying about his cows.

"Well, Rose dear," said Linnie, kindly, as she went into the room. "This is sad news again. You certainly are having a run of bad luck."

"It's too long a run," said Rose. "We shall be ruined – and all your money will be lost too, Peter."

"Oh, we're not ruined yet by a long way," said her brother-in-law, cheerfully – more cheerfully than he really felt. "It means harder work for a longer time – and maybe Cyril *will* have to leave school now, to help – because in my opinion that odd-job man isn't fit to work on a farm with that tummy trouble of his – and if Cyril takes his place, why, there's one wage saved!"

"I don't *wish* Cyril to leave school," said Rose, in her coldest voice. "It was a mistake coming here – a mistake coming into the country at all. I think we should leave and get a house in town somewhere – and David can get a job in some business. It seems quite obvious that we can't make this farm pay, and . . ."

"My *dear* Rose! You've only been here a few months!" said Peter. "What nonsense you talk! Wait till you've been here for five years before you say you can't make a farm pay."

140

"I don't intend to be here for even five months!" said Rose. "I hate it! It wasn't so bad when we had Ellen and Sally – but I can't seem to get anyone except that hateful Mrs Johns."

"Rose – Peter certainly can't afford to pay *two* women to run this little farmhouse," said Linnie. "I manage our big one with Dorcas alone – and you know how old and awkward it is, compared with yours. You'll have to make do with one, if you can get her."

"That decides me," said Rose, her voice shaking. "How could I ever manage with one – and only a country girl at that! What sort of life would it be for the children? What . . ."

"It would be exactly the same life as for *our* children!" said Linnie, getting cross. "They're happy enough – and so were yours when they lived with us. Shame on you, Rose! As soon as a little trouble comes, all you want to do is to run away, instead of facing it!"

"Have you ever *tried* facing troubles, Rose?" asked her brother-in-law, dryly. "No – you haven't. Well, I'll tell you what happens when you do – what *always* happens! They fade away – they get smaller and smaller – and then one day they're gone. But you have to face up to them and fight them. And that's what you never have done – and never will do it seems to me."

His brother David came into the room. "Hello, Linnie – well, Peter. It's good of you to come. Bad business this – ducks and hens nearly all gone – horse dying and six or eight cows going the same way!"

"To say nothing of Rose being no help to you at all!" said Peter. "Has she told you what *she* proposes?"

"No. What?" asked David, and turned to his wife.

"David, we're going to give up the farm, find a house – quite a little one, in town – and give up this dreadful life," said Rose, trying to speak calmly. "Cyril is not to leave

141

school and work on the farm. I wouldn't hear of it. Melisande can go to a nice school in town and so can Roderick. I don't like the schools here."

Her husband was too astonished to say a word. Rose went on, speaking quickly.

"I hate all this! I know we'll never do any good with Holly Farm. Why, we've failed already! We'll throw our hand in and leave while we can!"

"*We*?" said her husband. "And who do you mean by *we*, Rose?"

"All of us," said Rose. "You, me – the children."

"Count me out," said David, grimly. "I've got this farm and I'm keeping it. A bit of bad luck isn't going to knock *me* out! I've got Peter behind me too. And listen to this, Rose, because it's my last word – I'm a farmer, I'm going to remain one, and I'm sticking here!"

"Well – I'm *not*!" said Rose, her face going an angry red. "I shall leave you and take the children and go into town. I won't have them brought up like this."

"Oh Rose, Rose!" said Linnie, distressed. "These are dreadful things you are saying!"

"Be quiet!" said Rose, fiercely. "You think I ought to stay and slave like you do, don't you? Well . . ."

"That's enough, Rose," said David, looking suddenly angry. "If you had half the stuff in you that Linnie has, I wouldn't be sitting here feeling more ashamed of you tonight than I've ever felt ashamed of anyone in my life. You a wife! You a mother! You don't know how to be. You're neither wife nor mother – you're only Rose, pretty, spoilt Rose, who can't stick by her man, or look after her children!"

Rose flared up again. "How dare you talk to me like that! Where are the children? You'll soon see they prefer to go with me, than stay here on this horrible farm!"

"We'll fetch them," said Linnie, in a troubled voice. "I saw Cyril and Melisande in the dairy, as I came by."

142

They went to the dairy. Cyril and Melisande were still there, thankfully making the butter, which had come at last, into big pats. Melisande's face was thin and white, and her body was no longer plump. "Poor child!" thought Linnie, with a pang. "She's been doing all Rose's work as well as her own jobs. And Cyril looks worn out too. School and farmwork combined are too much for him."

"See how my pretty Melisande looks now, with all these things to do!" said Rose, angrily. "She's losing all her looks. I won't have it!"

They found Roddy in the kitchen, solemnly setting out the shoes he had cleaned. "What a good little boy!" thought Linnie. "And what a shame he couldn't have had that pup."

Susan had told her all about this, and she had felt angry. Roddy asked so little, and did so much. How could his mother have refused him such a little thing?

"And look at Roddy – slaving himself to death over jobs like this!" said his mother. Roddy looked up, surprised.

"Hello, Aunnt Linnie!" he said, pleased. "Look at the boots and shoes! I clean them just as well as Jack cleans them at Mistletoe Farm, don't I?"

Soon all three children were in the sitting room with their parents and their aunt and uncle. They looked in surprise at the grown ups. Why were they all so solemn?

"Children," said their father. "Your mother has put forward an idea. I want you to hear it and choose for yourselves what you want to do about it. Tell them, Rose."

"Well, my dears," said Rose, "I feel we can't go on with Holly Farm. I'm sure we shall always have bad luck. And it's much too hard work for me, and for all of you. Daddy wants Cyril to leave school and take the odd-job man's place. I don't want him to. Nor do I want you, Melisande, or you, Roddy, to slave as hard as you do – you,

143

Melisande, in the house, and you, Roddy, with the hens and other things. It's not fair."

She paused. All three children were listening intently. "So what I propose is this," said Rose. "I propose that we give up Holly Farm, and go back to the town life we know. Cyril will still go to school. We shall all have a much more comfortable and happy life, and we shall have learnt our lesson – the country is not for us!"

She stopped. Roddy stared solemnly at her. Then he looked at his father.

"Are you *really* thinking of leaving the farm already, Daddy?" he asked. "We've hardly come."

"No. I'm not leaving," said his father, steadily. "It's my farm and I'm stopping here to farm it. But if your mother wants a town-life she can have it, of course – without me. And I want you children to go with her, if you would like to. You can make your own free choice, and I shall respect it. You can always come here for weekends, of course."

Roddy went over to his father at once. "I'm staying here," he said. "You'll want *one* of us, won't you? I'm staying. I like the farm and all the jobs. Anyway I wouldn't run away from you like that, when things are bad!"

Linnie felt the tears come into her eyes. Was this the silly little mother's boy she had known nearly a year ago? How grown-up he sounded now.

"Very well. You shall stay with me on the farm," said his father, and put his arm round Roddy. He looked at Cyril.

"I expect you'd like to go with your mother," he said. "She'll need you."

Cyril hesitated. "She won't need me as much as you will, Dad," he said. "I don't like running away – and that's what it comes to. I'll be glad to leave school and come and work on the farm till things get better. I'd be a coward to desert the ship. I'll stay here."

And now it was Melisande's turn. She was torn in two. She felt sorry for her mother – but how much sorrier for her troubled father. "Who would look after you all and make Holly Farm a home for you, if Mother wasn't here?" she said. "I – I couldn't bear you just to have a housekeeper person. She couldn't make it home Mother, oh Mother – I'll *have* to stay with the others – you do see that, don't you? *Somebody's* got to look after them and make a home – and I can't bear a stranger to do that. I must stay – and I'll leave school as soon as I'm sixteen and stay home altogether. Things will be easier then."

An urgent knock sounded on the door just as Melisande finished speaking. Then the stockman's voice came.

"Mester Longfield, sir – come on up to the cows. They be right bad tonight!"

CHAPTER 24

Unexpected Friends

The two brothers rushed out of the house at once. Cyril followed. Linnie looked at Rose, who was crying pitifully in her chair. Melisande was trying to comfort her.

"Leave her alone, Melisande," said her aunt, wearily. "Nobody is stopping her from leaving, and living the life she longs for. She can see you all whenever she wants to. She has got her own way."

"I haven't, I haven't!" wept Rose. "I've lost my

145

husband and my children – nobody wants to come with me. I'm all alone."

"Well, don't go, then," said Roddy, sensibly and calmly. "I simply can't think what all the fuss is about, Mother. If you really want us all, stay with us. But you *don't* want us, actually, we're too much of a bother. I think it would be a very good idea if you had a lovely time in town and came to see us sometimes, like you used to do at Mistletoe Farm."

He went out of the room. "He doesn't love me a tiny bit," sobbed Rose." "And he used to be such a loving little boy."

"You shouldn't have sent that puppy of his away," said Linnie. "You spoilt his love for you then. He's a funny little boy. He'll never forgive you for that. Come, Rose, stop crying and go up to bed. I'll tidy round the kitchen a bit before I go. You go to bed too, Melisande, child – you look tired out."

"I am rather," said Melisande. She took Rose firmly up to bed and left her. She felt too tired to comfort her mother and listen to her grumbles that night.

Outside in the cowshed, the two Longfield brothers, the stockman and Cyril stood looking down at a moaning cow. Roddy peeped in at the half-open door, afraid to go any further in case he was sent out.

"If Twigg did that, he deserves to get imprisonment for life!" said David Longfield, between his teeth. "Poor creature – even those pills don't seem to have eased her."

"I don't believe Twigg could do this to animals," said his brother. "No, not even if he felt he had to revenge himself for a bitter insult. He might steal the hens and the ducks – I wouldn't put that past him – but he wouldn't damage stock."

Roddy listened in horror. However could *anyone* think Twigg would make the cows ill like that? They didn't know Twigg as he did, or they would never say such a thing.

His father suddenly saw him standing there, and, not wanting him to see the cow dying, sent him off at once.

Roddy obeyed. But he didn't want to go back to the house. It was a lovely night. He'd go for a walk – and for the first time for days he would take the imaginary Tinker with him for company!

He set off over the fields. He knew a hill where rabbits played at night. There would be enough moon to watch them by.

"Come on!" he said to Tinker. "Heel, now heel! No rabbit-hunting yet!"

When he got to the hillside he sat down, and the imaginary Tinker sat down too. Roddy could almost hear him panting. Then he very nearly jumped out of his skin!

It was *real* panting he heard. And it was real pattering feet he heard too. And now there was hot breath on the back of his neck, and a delighted wuff in his ear!

Roddy could hardly breathe. Surely – surely it wasn't his imaginary dog coming alive! A wet tongue licked his ear and two paws weighed down his shoulder. Roddy looked at this suddenly-materialised dog in wonder – yes – it was a golden spaniel, just as he had imagined Tinker to be.

Then a voice came from the bushes. "Mr Potts. Where are you?"

Roddy leapt up a if he had been shot. Why – it was Twigg – and this dog was not his imaginary Tinker come alive, it was Mr Potts, Twigg's own golden spaniel.

"Twigg! Twigg! Where are you? It's me, Roddy."

Two shadows detached themselves from the blackness of the hedge. They were Twigg and Tommy Lane. "What you doing here this time of night?" demanded Twigg.

"Never mind that. Twigg – did you know Daddy's cows were dying?" said Roddy.

"I did," said Twigg, grimly. "And seemingly, 'cording to old Potts, I'm the one that killed them."

"That's silly, Twigg," said Roddy. "You couldn't

possibly harm a cow. *I* know that. But I know something else too."

"What's that, young sir?" said Twigg.

"I know that if anyone in this world could keep them alive, you could keep them alive, you could, Twigg," said Roddy, earnestly. "Please, Twigg – come and see them. One's groaning dreadfully."

"Well – mebbe I know what's wrong with your cows," said Twigg, in a suddenly grim voice. "Mebbe me and Tommy Lane have been after them what did the damage – and mebbe we've got out of them what it was . . ."

"And mebbe we knows as how to cure 'em," chimed in Tommy Lane's voice. "But we won't. Folks as send the police after us don't deserve no help."

"Perhaps we don't," said Roddy, desperately. "But the *cows* deserve it. They're good cows, Twigg – you've seen them."

"Ay. I've seen them," said Twigg. "Here, Mr Potts, to heel. We've got work to do tonight. We're going along to undeserving folks and we're going to do them a right good turn – all alonga this here pest of a boy!"

"Oh Twigg – thank you," said Roddy, and hung on to Twigg's arm in sudden heartfelt gratitude.

They didn't say much as they made their way, the four of them (counting Mr Potts the spaniel), over the fields to Holly Farm. They came to the cowsheds, which were still lighted by a lantern. A groaning noise came to their ears.

"Now you go back to the house, Master Roddy," said Twigg, stopping outside the cowshed door. "There's things to be done as isn't fit for young eyes to see – t'would only worrit you, and get into your dreams. You go to bed – and if things go well, you'll know it soon enough."

Roddy squeezed Twigg's arm and set off obediently. Twigg and Lane went into the shed, much to the amazement of the Longfield brothers and of the stockman there.

Many hours later five very tired men stumbled out of the sheds. One cow had died – but all the rest were saved. The horse was all right too – it would soon take a turn for the better and be fit for work in a week.

"I don't know exactly what you did, Twigg," said David Longfield. "Your hands are as quick and deft as the paws of a cat – but all I can say is, you've worked miracles. God bless you, man – you've got the free run of my land for all the time I farm it – and Tommy Lane too. I'll never forgot tonight."

"Thank you kindly sir," said Twigg, a grin stretching his leathery face. "That's young Master Roddy got me here tonight. Pity about that pup, sir – he were right down pleased with it. Tommy Lane here has kep' it, just in case. Does your heart good to see a young-un like Master Roddy."

"Yes. Chip of the old block – like your son Master Jack, sir," said Tommy Lane to Peter Longfield. "Well good-night, and the best of luck, sir – and if you want some of your hens and ducks, you'll find them with the gypsies over to Whortleberry Hill – if they're still there tomorrow!"

"What!" cried David Longfield, in astonishment. "How do you know?"

"Well, me and Tommy here, we didn't like old Potts the policeman coming after us with tales of stolen hens and ducks, like," said Twigg. "Nor didn't we like them tales of damaging cows and horses, sir. So we ups and goes to find them what does do these rascally things – the gypsies who lived on your bit of common till the day afore yesterday."

"The gypsies!" said David and Peter together and the stockman grunted. "But they've gone," said David.

"Yes – I told you, they're over to Whortleberry Hill," said Twigg. "You turned 'em off you land, sir, and you miscalled them and set the dogs on them – quite right too,

149

they'm rascally folks, not like us honest poachers. Well, they're spiteful, sir, – and before they went, they took your ducks and hens – and damaged your cows. They damaged that horse of yourn too, and the other cows, no doubt of that. You set that bossy old policeman after them gypsies, sir. They've got your ducks and hens running about still, under their caravans. And mebbe you'll find other things belonging to you *inside* the vans. You set old Potts after them gypsies!"

"I will," said David Longfield, grimly.

"And tell that policeman I'll be waiting at home all tomorrow to accept his apologies," said Twigg, maliciously. "You tell him that from old Twigg. Goodnight to you, sirs."

He and Tommy Lane and Mr Potts the spaniel melted into the shadows. David gave a sigh. "Well – he's done a good night's work for me, has old Twigg. I wonder what's happened to poor old Linnie all this time!"

They went back to Holly Farm. There was a light burning in the sittingroom but otherwise the house was in darkness. The men got themselves something to eat and drink. The door opened softly as they sat silently at the table.

It was Rose. Rose with swollen cheeks and swollen eyes – a very subdued and miserable Rose.

"I waited up for you," she whispered. "Linnie went home in the car. Are the cows better?"

"Yes. They'll be all right now," said David, wearily. "Peter, will you sleep on the sofa?"

"I've made up the bed in Ellen's room for him," said Rose, and she took him up. He said a curt goodnight to her and shut the door. She went down to David.

"Well, Rose, you made a poor show of yourself tonight," said her husband, "but we'll say no more now. Go to bed. I'm going to sleep down here. I'm too tired to undress."

"I just want to say one thing," said Rose. "I'm not going to leave Holly Farm either, David. I'm sticking by you too. I

150

can never be as good a wife and mother as Linnie – but I'll be a second-best, if you can put up with that."

"Bless you, Rose," said David, smiling for the first time that day. "That's the best news I've had for a long time – and I'm too tired to talk about it! Too tired even to tell you I love you just as much, and we'll begin all over again!"

Rose kissed him and went upstairs by herself. David was asleep before she had got to her bedroom door! In Ellen's room Peter was fast asleep too.

Rose got into bed. She had heard a lot of things from Linnie that night after the men had gone out to the cows – hard things, straight things, terrible things. And then Linnie had got into the car and driven away and left Rose to her own thoughts.

She had gone to Melisande, but Melisande had not changed her mind about sticking to the farm. Neither had Cyril. She had not attempted to go to Roddy.

She couldn't bear to be alone, in a town house all by herself! She knew that. But sticking to Holly Farm meant discomfort and unpleasant things and hard work. She had given her children the choice and they had chosen the hard way. She was the only weak one of the family – and they could quite well do without her.

But Rose, staring into the darkness, knew that she couldn't do without *them*. She couldn't. And now she would somehow have to make them feel they couldn't do without her either, and that would be very hard. David loved her – she would soon win him back. Cyril thought the world of her – it wouldn't be very difficult to get *his* love back once more.

And she would win back Melisande too – she would even get up at half-past six every morning, so that her children shouldn't have to come down and get their own breakfasts! What a tremendous resolve for poor Rose.

She would ask advice from Linnie and Dorcas and follow it. And what about Roddy?

Roddy didn't like her any more. She knew that he didn't. He was cold to her – all the lovely warmth of feeling he had once had for her was gone. It would be very very difficult to win Roddy back.

Yes – that certainly would be difficult, the most imposs- ible task of all – and there was only one sure way of doing it. *David* knew what it was, but he wasn't going to tell Rose. She would have to think it out for herself!

CHAPTER 25

A Proper Family Again

The next day dawned bright and clear. The cock crowed loudly as he always did. David Longfield awoke with a jump, stiff and tired after his night on the sofa. He glanced at the clock. Half-past six!

He heard his brother coming down the stairs – and then he heard somebody in the kitchen. "Surely not Melisande down already!" he thought.

"No – it wasn't – it was actually Rose! Rose with eyes still red, and a very tired face, but an astonishingly cheerful Rose. "I'm just getting you something to eat," she said. "The kettle's almost boiling. Don't go out till you've had something."

Peter was astonished. He didn't know that Rose had completely changed her mind. "What a pity she isn't always like this!" he thought.

The men went out to the cowshed. Rose rushed round

doing this and that. She was very tired, but she was no longer miserable.

Melisande was astonished beyond words when she came down. So was Cyril.

"Don't look so surprised," said Rose. "I've changed my mind about leaving you and the farm. *I'm* staying too. It seems as if you could all have done without *me* – but I find I can't do without *you*!"

The children were more touched than they showed. They gave her a hug, and Cyril whispered in her ear. "I'm glad, Mother, awfully glad!"

They told Roddy when he came down a little later. "Mother's not leaving us, after all. She's sticking to the farm."

"Oh," said Roddy, not sounding in the least interested. He was much more interested in wondering how the cows were!

They caught the bus to school as usual. It had been arranged that Cyril should finish his week out and then go on to the farm – at least till this bad spell had passed.

They came home at tea time, wondering what news there was. The bus was late and it was a quarter-past five before they stepped off it at the bottom of the lane. They ran up to the farm.

They passed the farmhouse window, and peered inside. "My goodness!" said Melisande, startled, "someone's laid hightea – cheese and ham and all! I could do with it too – we're so late."

"Well, if it's high tea I'll come in too," said Roddy, who usually collected his tray and shot off to the henhouse by himself.

Melisande went to find her mother. She was in the kitchen, making the tea. Melisande stared at her in surprise, for she was wearing something she had never seen her in before!

153

"Mother! You've got my overall on!" she said. "Oh Mother, it's so *peculiar* to see you in that – but you look nice and homey. I like it. Let me help you."

"No. It's all done," said Rose, looking flushed and young again. "We'll all have tea together. I can hear Daddy coming in too."

In five minutes time the family were sitting down to a really good high tea, "just like Mistletoe Farm" as Roddy noticed with satisfaction. Melisande and Cyril were very happy, and their father laughed at their jokes. Only Roddy was stolid and silent as usual, and barely said thank you to his mother for passing him his tea.

"You know that we're *all* sticking together at Holly Farm, don't you?" his father said, wondering if Roddy knew. "You know that, don't you, Roddy? Mother too."

"Yes. Cyril told me this morning," said Roddy, not looking up.

"Roddy! Aren't you *glad* Mother's not going away to town?" said Melisande.

"Well – it wouldn't have made much difference," said Roddy. "Not to me, I mean. Mother didn't really bother much about me or what I wanted – did you. Mother?"

"Don't talk like that, Roddy," said his father, ashamed of him.

"Sorry," said Roddy, and munched at his bread and cheese.

The telephone rang. Melisande went to it and came back glowing. "Oh Mother! That was Dorcas – and what do you think – she says Sally's just been to see her and she doesn't like her new place, and Dorcas has told her to come back to Holly Farm!"

"Good!" said Cyril, Roddy and their father together. Rose beamed. "Is that really true, Melisande! Oh, I must tell Dorcas how glad I am!"

Dorcas was cautious over the telephone. She knew that

154

Mrs David, as she called her, had turned over a new leaf and was going to try and be sensible – but she wasn't going to be too friendly to her till she knew if she was going to keep it up!

"Yes, Ma'am," she said. "Sally's here now. She can't come for two weeks, Ma"m, but you'll manage till then, I don't doubt. Yes, Ma'am, I'll tell Sally you're very pleased. Yes, she's not a bad girl, Sally Goodbye, Ma'am."

Then the table talk turned to the cows. Except for that one that had died, all of them were now on the mend. The shire horse had actually stood on his feet. Mr Longfield looked a different man that evening.

"Well, well!" he said. "Cows on the mend, old Blackie getting better, Sally coming back – what more do we want? Seems as if our luck is turning at last!"

Rose suddenly thought of what her brother-in-law, Peter, had said the night before. "Face up to troubles, and they'll melt away – but you've got to face up to them first."

There was the sound of footsteps coming up to the front door and then a peremptory rat-a-tat-tat. Melisande went to answer it. It was Mr Potts.

"Your father in, Miss?" he said. "Ah, good evening to you, sir. Er – acting on advice from Mr Sam Twigg, I went over to them gypsies at Whortleberry Hill, sir – the ones that camped on your common some time back – and there I found the hens and ducks, I've set down on this list, sir."

He presented Mr Longfield with a neatly written list. "Mr Twigg, sir, he tells me they belong to you – the ones that were reported stolen."

"The ones you thought he stole," said Roddy's disapproving voice. "I always knew he didn't."

"I have – er – apprehended these here poultry, sir," went on the ponderous Mr Potts. "They're at the police-station, along with a few other things of yours, and on your recognizing the same as your property I should be pleased if you would remove them forthwith."

"And I should be more than pleased to do so, Potts," said Mr Longfield, delighted. "I never thought I'd get any of those back."

"Well, sir," you were lucky," said the policeman. "I reckon the gypsies have eaten about eight of the hens and ducks sir, – but they couldn't manage the lot. Probably they meant to sell them."

Mr Potts departed. Mr Longfield went back to the table, rubbing his hands. "Another bit of luck I didn't expect," he said. "Well, Rose dear, I must get the car out and 'remove my property from the police station forthwith' as Mr Potts puts it."

"I bet he was wild when he found that it was the gypsies who stole the hens and damaged the cows and not Twigg," said Roddy. "And he'll be wilder still when Twigg tells him he can poach all he likes on Mistletoe Farm and on Holly Farm too!"

"David! I just want to ask you to bring something back for me in the car," suddenly said Rose, and she slipped out after him. She looked back to see if any of the children were listening, and then whispered in his ear.

He caught her to him and gave her a hug. "Bless you, Rose – that was the last lovely thing left that could happen. I'll bring it, don't you fear."

He drove off in the car. Soon the tea was being cleared. Roddy went out to grade and wash the eggs as usual. He whistled to his imaginary Tinker.

"Everybody's happy," he informed Tinker. "Every-thing's come right. Wag your tail, Tinker. But let me whisper something to you. I still can't forgive Mother for what she did about that pup!"

He finished the eggs and went indoors to wash. He

heard his father's voice in the kitchen. "Did you bring back the hens, Dad?" called Roddy.

"Yes," called back his father. "Only seven ducks and hens are missing. One of them laid an egg in the car coming back – and two of them laid eggs for Mr Potts in the police station."

"Come out here, Roddy!" called his mother. "Something else came with the hens."

Roddy went out to the kitchen. He went in at the door and then stood transfixed. His mother was holding something in her hands – something that cuddled against her and squealed.

"Mother," said Roddy, and took a step forward. He could hardly believe his eyes. It was his pup – the little spaniel pup he had taken back to Tommy Lane – the very same one.

"Here you are, Roddy – it's yours," said his mother, in a warm voice. "I was silly to think I wouldn't like it. It's perfectly sweet. I shall love to look after it when you're at school. It's just as nice as Crackers."

"Nicer," said Roddy. He took the tiny squirming creature and held it against his neck. It tried to get down his shirt. "Tinker!" said Roddy, happily, squeezing it gently. "You really *are* a tinker!"

"Mother told me to bring it back for you," said his father. "I was so pleased."

"You're a darling, Mother, and I love you!" said Roddy, his heart overflowing with joy. He gave his mother such a hug that she squealed like the puppy. "It's the nicest present in the world."

"The best bit of luck you've had for a long time, Roddy!" said his father. "But you deserve it."

Roddy beamed at his father and mother as he fondled the squirming pup. "Looks as if we're a proper family again, doesn't it, Dad?" he said.

It does indeed, Roddy – and long may you be happy with Tinker and all the rest at Holly Farm!

Have you read all the adventures in the "Mystery" series by Enid Blyton?

The Rockingdown Mystery

Roger, Diana, Snubby and Barney hear strange noises in the cellar while staying at Rockingdown Hall. Barney goes to investigate and makes a startling discovery . . .

The Rilloby Fair Mystery

Valuable papers have disappeared – the Green Hands Gang has struck again! Which of Barney's workmates at the circus is responsible? The four friends turn detectives – and have to tackle a dangerous criminal.

The Ring O'Bells Mystery

Eerie things happen at deserted Ring O'Bells Hall – bells start to ring, strange noises are heard in a secret passage, and there are some very unfriendly strangers about. Something very mysterious is going on and the friends mean to find out what . . .

The Rubadub Mystery

Who is the enemy agent at the top-secret submarine harbour? Roger, Diana, Snubby and Barney are determined to find out – and find themselves involved in a most exciting mystery.

The Rat-A-Tat Mystery

When the big knocker on the ancient door of Rat-A-Tat House bangs by itself in the middle of the night, it heralds a series of very peculiar happenings – and provides another action-packed adventure for Roger, Diana, Snubby and Barney.

The Ragamuffin Mystery

"This is going to be the most exciting holiday we've ever had," said Roger – and little does he know how true his words will prove when he and his three friends go to Merlin's Cove and discover the hideout of a gang of thieves.

Armada

THE MYSTERY THAT NEVER WAS

by

Enid Blyton

Don't miss this exciting adventure story by the world's best-ever storyteller!

Nicky decides to invent a mystery for his Uncle Bob — a private investigator — to solve. But there's a nasty shock in store for Nicky. When spooky lights signal in the night from the old mansion on Skylark Hill, he realises that his mystery is coming horrifyingly true.

Armada

THE ENID BLYTON TRUST
FOR CHILDREN

We hope you have enjoyed the adventures of the children in this book. Please think for a moment about those children who are too ill to do the exciting things you and your friends do.

Help them by sending a donation, large or small to the ENID BLYTON TRUST FOR CHILDREN. The Trust will use all your gifts to help children who are sick or handicapped and need to be made happy and comfortable.

Please send your postal orders or cheques to:

> The Enid Blyton Trust for Children,
> 3rd Floor,
> New South Wales House,
> 15 Adam Street,
> London WC2N 6AA

Thank you very much for your help.